# A Great Idea!

We have selected some of the novels
of Harlequin's world-famous authors
and combined them in a 3-in-1 Omnibus series.

You get THREE enjoyable, full-length romances,
complete and unabridged,
by the same author,
in ONE deluxe, paperback volume,
every month.

# A Great Value!

Almost 600 pages of pure entertainment
for an unbelievably low price,

ONLY $1.95.

A truly "Jumbo" read,
available wherever paperback books are sold.

# WELCOME

# TO THE WONDERFUL WORLD

# OF *Harlequin Romances!*

Interesting, informative and entertaining,
each Harlequin Romance portrays an appealing
and original love story. With a varied array
of settings, we may lure you on an African safari,
to a quaint Welsh village, or an exotic riviera
location — anywhere and everywhere that adventurous
men and women fall in love.

As publishers of Harlequin Romances, we're
extremely proud of our books. Since 1949,
Harlequin Enterprises has built its publishing
reputation on the solid base of quality and
originality. Our stories are the most popular
paperback romances sold in North America; every
month, eight new titles are released and sold at
nearly every book-selling store in Canada and the
United States

A free catalogue listing all available Harlequin Romances
can be yours by writing to the

HARLEQUIN READER SERVICE,
(In the U.S.): M.P.O. Box 707, Niagara Falls, N.Y. 14302
(In Canada): Stratford, Ontario, Canada. N5A 6W4

or use order coupon at back of books.

We sincerely hope you enjoy reading
this Harlequin Romance.

Yours truly,

THE PUBLISHERS
   *Harlequin Romances*

# THE GARDEN
# OF DREAMS

by

## SARA CRAVEN

HARLEQUIN BOOKS    TORONTO
WINNIPEG

Original hard cover edition published in 1975
by Mills & Boon Limited


SBN 373-01943-2


Harlequin edition published January 1976

Printed in Canada

# CHAPTER ONE

'ARE you going to marry him?' said Jenny, straight to the point as usual.

'I don't know.' Lissa Fairfax lifted the brooch from its satin bed in the worn velvet box, with a troubled frown. The late afternoon sun was pouring in through the big window of the living room of their small flat and catching the gleaming stones, as she turned the brooch in her hand, and the sparkling facets gleamed like living fire.

She sighed a little. 'One thing is certain. This will have to go back.'

'I don't see why,' argued Jenny. 'Paul has given you masses of presents. You've never thought twice about accepting any of them before.'

'But this is different.' Lissa examined the brooch, her frown deepening. 'This is valuable—I'm sure it is. Look at the colour of the gold, and the way the clasp is made. It looks very old.'

'Perhaps he's showering you with the family heirlooms,' said Jenny. 'Still, it makes a nice change from flowers and perfume, and those gorgeous chocolates that we didn't dare eat because of that diet thing we were on. Oh—and that super lighter. I'd forgotten that.'

'I hadn't.' Lissa put the brooch back in the case. 'That was too expensive as well. It's all too much, too soon, Jen. After all, I've only known him six weeks.'

'Some people would say that was long enough.'

'Well, I wouldn't.' Lissa's tone was definite. 'I want to know someone far better than that before spending the rest of my life with them. I don't like being rushed

5

into things.'

Jenny sighed elaborately. 'The most attractive Frenchman I've ever seen, young and wealthy—yes, he is, Lissa—no one could have his sort of clothes or car unless they were loaded, and he wants to marry you. And instead of falling into his arms, you say...'

'I'll think it over.' Lissa smiled at her flatmate affectionately. They had been together ever since she had come to London, sharing this upstairs flatlet of sitting room, tiny bedroom with enough space for two beds and a Victorian-style wardrobe, with a kitchenette and tiny bathroom. 'I mean to think it over very seriously. After all, you knew Roger for ages before you even thought of settling down. I can't just grab Paul and let everything go by the board. After all, what do I really know about him—about his family or his background?'

'Hasn't he ever mentioned anyone?'

'He's spoken of his mother a few times—and he's made odd references to a brother. I got the impression there might be a spot of friction there. He didn't say so, of course.'

'Your womanly intuition told you so.' Jenny turned back to the neglected ironing board and began to pay minute attention to the cuffs of a white silk blouse. 'Honestly, love, he's the catch of the year, and he's just waiting to drop into your hands. And you get on so well together. You can't deny that.'

'Oh, yes, he's wonderful to go out with—charming, attentive, amusing—everything anyone could wish, but——' Lissa paused.

Jenny raised her eyes to the ceiling. 'The girl wants jam on it. Okay, but what?'

'But I can't see him married and settling down to a routine just yet. Take that job of his at the Embassy. He doesn't care about it at all.'

6

'Well, if he's as wealthy as he seems to be, there's no real need for him to worry.'

'No, but if you have a job, you should do it, not just play at it.' Lissa stared down at the brooch. 'And now this. I wish I knew where he'd got it from.'

'You surely don't think he nicked it?' Jenny was horrified.

Lissa laughed. 'Of course not. But it's so uncharacteristic of Paul. He's such a present-day person, and this has definitely an air of days gone by.'

'Show it to Maggie,' Jenny suggested. 'After all, what's the good of being a secretary to a historical novelist if you can't pick her brains occasionally?'

'She might know, I suppose,' Lissa said slowly. 'I still think the best thing is to give it back to Paul when I see him tonight.'

'Do you think tonight he'll want a definite answer?' Jenny asked.

'I doubt it,' said Lissa. 'We're going to a party, one of those formal things at the Embassy, I think. Still, it will give me a chance to wear my new chiffon.'

'It would also give you a chance to wear the brooch,' Jenny said, grinning.

Lissa shook her head decisively. 'No. I'm just going to give it back to him and explain that I can't accept expensive presents like this when I've only known him such a short time.'

'Even though he wants to marry you?' Jenny asked.

'Particularly because of that. You know what they say about marrying in haste,' said Lissa. 'After all, think how many years you've known Roger, and you went out with him for at least a year before he even suggested an engagement.'

Jenny laughed. 'But Roger, bless him, isn't a glamorous young Frenchman who wanted to sweep me off my feet.'

'I don't think I want to be swept either,' Lissa said reflectively, 'and if I do, I'm not sure this is the way I would want it done. The fact is I don't know what I do want. I've never felt so unsure.'

'I'd say it was spring fever, only spring's over now really,' said Jenny. She picked up the brooch again, and examined it minutely. 'I suppose the stones must be zircons. They're certainly big ones.'

'They couldn't be diamonds could they?' Lissa gasped, horrified. 'I wonder if the French have some strange habit of giving brooches instead of engagement rings.'

They both bent, placing the brooch against the glittering three-diamond ring on Jenny's engagement finger, and studying the two closely.

Jenny shook her head. 'It must be zircons. I mean, there just aren't diamonds that big any more, and the cutting looks different too. But it's an antique, and no mistake.'

'I don't doubt it,' Lissa said a little despondently. 'The problem now is how to return it gracefully.'

'Your main problem at the moment is getting ready for the big night out,' said Jenny. 'I don't know what time Paul is calling for you, but the immersion heater's been on for ages.'

'Heavens!' Lissa glanced at her watch. 'I had no idea it was so late. I must fly!'

Some ten minutes later, her fair hair pinned into a topknot, Lissa lay luxuriating in hot scented water. She ignored the fact that time was pressing and closing her eyes against the steam, let the worries of the day, including this latest one, slowly submerge. Margaret Desmond, her employer, was one of the most charming people alive and by no means a slavedriver, but when the idea for a new book was paramount with her she demanded total concentration, and Lissa had to acknowledge that since Paul's proposal two nights earlier, she had been unable to keep her mind wholly on the job in hand.

Although, as she reminded herself with slightly rueful amusement, the new book had been the means of her meeting Paul in the first place.

Maggie was currently engaged on researching background for a novel about the French Revolution and Lissa had been sent to the French Embassy to collect a promised list of reference books and biographies of the period from an eminent French historian, with whom Maggie had been in correspondence, and who was staying in London for a few days.

Her note of introduction had been handed in the first instance to Paul, whose job it had been to conduct her through a bewildering array of corridors to the suite being occupied by the historian. By some strange coincidence, and somewhat to Lissa's relief, he was still waiting when she emerged, and not only conducted her back to the foyer, but insisted on driving her back to Maggie's flat in his low-slung and very expensive sports car.

Maggie had received him amiably, offered him her special sherry, and allowed him to stay for lunch, presiding over the meal with the benign air of an inveterate matchmaker. That was one of the drawbacks of working for your own godmother, Lissa reflected. Maggie was too apt very often to take rather a personal interest in one's off-duty moments, but Lissa knew that it was precisely this fact that gave her parents, hundreds of miles away in Devon, such a sense of reassurance.

Maggie was quick to see romance even in the most unlikely situations, which perhaps explained the extreme popularity of her books, and it was obvious that Paul had her approval as a suitor for Lissa.

'I daren't tell her that he's proposed to me.' Lissa thought, 'or she'll write off to Mother and Dad and the wedding will be planned before I know it.'

Madame de Gue. She said the name slowly, trying to relate it to herself, and giggled. It sounded alien and unreal.

And if she did marry Paul, where would they live? In France? Lissa's French was fairly fluent, especially with some recent coaching from Paul, but it was still on a pretty schoolgirl level, as she was the first to admit. Paul himself spoke almost perfect English, but he would have relatives, no doubt, who might not be bi-lingual.

She got out of the bath and began to dry herself. 'If I really loved him,' she thought, 'I wonder if I would be having all these doubts. I'd know that loving him was enough, and would get us across all the bridges as we came to them.'

Physically he stirred her as no other man she had ever met had done, but she was uncertain whether this was due to genuine feeling, or was merely the reaction of a fairly inexperienced girl to what she suspected was a very experienced young man. Lissa grimaced. Again, it all seemed like a game to Paul, she thought, and she wondered if she had given in to his desires, whether he would still want to marry her now.

It was not a particularly pleasant thought, and she pushed it away resolutely. Give Paul his due, he had always insisted that her instinctive recoil from his passion delighted him.

The permissive society, he had made it clear, while enjoyable, did not extend to the woman he wanted to make his wife. Although Lissa had no desire to become part of the permissive society, this typically masculine attitude had annoyed her.

'That's a mediaeval way of looking at it,' she had

10

protested to him once.

He laughed. 'But it is true, *chérie*, and all men feel it in their hearts, even if it is no longer fashionable to say so aloud. The girls they marry must be for them alone. And I assure you that my attitude is positively enlightened compared with—let us say—my brother.'

Lissa stared at him. 'So, if I had slept with another man, you wouldn't want me?'

'I did not say that, my beautiful Lissa, but I would naturally feel—differently.'

Lissa had always felt a spirit of rebellion rise within her at this attitude. She was no women's libber.

'But he must learn that he doesn't own me,' she told herself.

She fastened the belt of her housecoat and padded into the bedroom. Her skin was naturally pale, but flawless, and she applied only light make-up, using eye-shadow to flatter the slightly tip-tilted grey-green eyes that were her loveliest feature. She brushed her long, almost silver-blonde hair until it shone, before winding it deftly into a smooth elegant coil at the back of her head, with just two curling tendrils allowed to escape and frame her face. The chiffon dress, a floating cloud of misty blues, greens and violet hung from the wardrobe door. It was a dress she particularly liked and Jenny called it her 'sea nymph' look. Some nymph, Lissa thought, slipping her feet into high-heeled silver shoes. She hoped that Paul would approve. It was the first time she had ever worn it for him, but she had got the impression that the party tonight was an important one and she was determined to look her best. She was used by now to the photographers with their flash-lamps who attended these affairs, and had frequently been the subject of their attentions, although she had never seen any pictures of herself actually featured anywhere. She guessed they would mainly be of interest to French magazines.

When she was ready, she sprayed on some of her favourite scent, and stood back and looked at herself in the long mirror that she and Jenny had found in an old junk shop, and cleaned and polished up.

Her skin gleamed against the deep V of the neckline and the full skirts floated out like cobweb as she turned.

Jenny appeared in the doorway, holding the box with the brooch.

'Gorgeous,' she said appreciatively. 'And this brooch would just be the finishing touch, you know.' She held it against herself. 'Look what it does for this old black jumper. And just think what it would do for the chiffon! Try it on at least, there's no harm in that.'

'I suppose not.' Lissa took the brooch and pinned it at her neckline. Gleaming there, it seemed to reflect back every sensuous colour in the gown, and she stared at it longingly.

'Oh, Lissa, you must wear it. It looks wonderful,' Jenny pleaded.

Lissa nodded ruefully, but as her hands went up to unfasten it, the door bell rang.

'That'll be Paul.' Lissa swirled across the tiny bedroom and across the living room to the door and flung it open. She dropped in a mock curtsy. *'Bonsoir, monsieur.'*

*'Bonsoir, mademoiselle.'*

The right answer. The wrong voice. Lissa looked up for the first time and found herself confronting a complete stranger. He was tall and very dark. His hair was black and his thin face was tanned. The expression in his low-lidded eyes as he stood looking down at Lissa was unreadable, but a faint smile played without warmth about his firm mouth.

There was something vaguely objectionable in the

way he was looking her over, and Lissa lifted her chin and stared back.

·'You must forgive me, *monsieur*. As must have been obvious, I was expecting someone else.'

'That is why I am here.' He took an envelope from his pocket and handed it to her. It bore her name and she tore it open with a feeling of anxiety. Inside was a typewritten note from Paul.

'Lissa, *chérie*, forgive me, but I cannot make it to the party tonight. Something totally unexpected has cropped up, and I am obliged to change my plans. I will see you tomorrow instead and make up for it, I swear. Your loving Paul.'

'I am sorry to be the bearer of bad news.' The stranger's voice did not sound particularly regretful. 'Paul was unable to come himself to explain, and of course you have no telephone, so I was happy to oblige him.'

'Thank you, *monsieur*.' In spite of her bitter disappointment Lissa did not forget her manners. 'Won't you come in for a moment? I am Lissa Fairfax as you have already guessed, and this is my flatmate Jenny Caldwell.'

He stepped into the living room, and stood looking at the small room with its clutter of easy chairs, and the small sofa before the gas fire. His expression gave nothing away, but Lissa could guess that he was not impressed.

'You have not told us your name, *monsieur*,' she reminded him a little. tartly, and he turned, giving her another of those sweeping looks from head to foot that she was beginning to find so disconcerting.

'I am Raoul Denis, at your service, *mademoiselle*.' His dark eyes considered her again. 'Now that I have seen you I can understand why Paul should be so *bouleversé* at having to sacrifice his evening with you.'

He paused. 'I have a proposition for you, *mademoiselle*. I too have suffered the same fate this evening. My partner has been suddenly overtaken by illness, and I have a cocktail party to attend, with the theatre afterwards. As we have both been left in the lurch, shall we take advantage of the situation and spend the evening together?'

Lissa stared at him. 'But I don't know you,' she exclaimed. 'Paul has never mentioned a Raoul Denis to me. Are you close friends?'

He shrugged. 'Let us say we have been acquaintances for a very long time—and he did trust me to come here and deliver this note. And it would be a tragedy to waste that gown and all that radiance at home, when all the world is waiting. And you need have no fears. Paul would not be jealous of me.'

'For your information, *monsieur*, Paul has no real right to be jealous of anyone,' Lissa said a little coldly.

She looked at Raoul Denis in some perplexity. It was true. She was all dressed up, with nowhere to go, and his alternative suggestion was appealing.

At last she spoke. 'Very well, *monsieur*. I shall be happy to be your companion. If you will just allow me to fetch my wrap.'

She walked back into the bedroom, and closed the door. Jenny was sitting on one of the beds, staring at her.

'You have all the luck!' she exclaimed. 'If that had been Roger, I would have been condemned to an evening's television.'

'I don't know.' Lissa took her black velvet coat out of the wardrobe, and checked over the contents of her silver kid purse. 'He seems polite enough, and if he knows Paul, I suppose that must make him respectable. But I can't understand his invitation.'

14

'Why not?' Jenny was intrigued. 'He's an absolute dish.'

'Yes,' Lissa said slowly, 'I suppose he is. But all the time he was talking to me, though he was civil enough, I felt there was something there. That he didn't really like me. That there was something—just slightly wrong about the whole thing.'

'I think you have too vivid an imagination,' Jenny said decisively. 'I think it's a most sensible solution. You're both on your own. Why not take advantage of each other's company? If you don't like him, you don't have to talk to him all the time. You're going to the theatre, remember.'

'Yes, I suppose you're right. I'm just being a fool.' Lissa put on her coat and gasped, 'I'd forgotten—the heirloom! What am I going to do with it this evening? Where can I hide it?' She gazed round the room, a little desperately. 'There's nowhere really safe.'

'Well, it hardly seems worth building a strongroom just for my Indian necklace and your copper bracelet that Aunt Rosemary sent to ward off rheumatism,' said Jenny. 'If you're worried about it, leave it where it is. It looks good there. I think Monsieur Thing thinks so too. I noticed him giving it a keen glance as he came in.'

'It seems wrong to wear it, when I meant to give it back tonight.'

'Well, at least you'll have the comfort of knowing exactly where it is,' argued Jenny. 'And Paul will never know.'

'I suppose you're right,' Lissa agreed. 'And to be honest, I like the way it looks.' She fastened the silver clasps on her coat. 'I'm not looking forward to this evening. He seems rather a chilly mortal.'

'Unlike Monsieur Paul de Gue, for instance,' Jenny said mischievously. 'I've got a feeling that Paul will live to bless this evening. Seriously, doesn't the Pirate King out there remind you of someone?'

'I don't think so.' Lissa took a last look in the mirror. 'Who were you thinking of?'

'I don't know. Just for a second—as you opened the door—he looked familiar.'

'It can only have been for a second. I don't think familiarity is his strong point. In fact I'm expecting to be turned into a pillar of ice as the evening wears on,' Lissa said drily.

On her return to the living room, she found Monsieur Denis standing by the small sideboard looking at a glossy magazine. It was one of their landlady's few personal indulgences that she liked reading magazines that showed 'how the other half live', as she put it, and she always passed these magazines on to the girls and seemed disappointed that they were not more interested in the gala evenings and hunt balls that were largely featured.

This particular magazine had been pushed under the door when the girls came home from work with a note attached: 'Wait till you see this'. Neither of them had even scanned through it, however, because Paul's parcel with the brooch had also been delivered.

'Don't tell me,' Jenny had commented, picking the magazine up from the carpet. 'Her favourite deb's just got herself engaged to her favourite chinless wonder.'

As Lissa entered, Raoul Denis flung the magazine down and turned towards her. She was startled to encounter a sudden blaze of anger in his eyes, but before she could fully assimilate this, or begin to wonder at the reason, it had faded, and the mask of rather enigmatic aloofness had returned.

Lissa smiled rather more cheerfully than she actually felt. She wished now that she had turned down his invitation and spent the evening by the fire with a book. He hardly seemed likely to turn into a boon companion from what she had seen of him so far.

'I'm quite ready, *monsieur*.' She turned to Jenny, who was standing behind her. ''Bye, love, have a wonderful time at Roger's. I suppose you'll be spending the night there.'

'Well, his mother is full of wedding talk and lists into the small hours, so I might as well take a nightie and a toothbrush,' Jenny said, smiling.

'I'll see you tomorrow evening, then. Don't forget, it's my turn to do the shopping.'

'Yes, but I'll willingly do it, if you're going out with Paul.' Jenny began, but she was interrupted by the incisive voice of Monsieur Denis.

'Time is running short, *mademoiselle*. I suggest you reserve these domestic details for another occasion.'

Lissa kept her temper in check. After all, he was a friend of Paul's, but she could feel the colour burning in her cheek as she went to the door. 'Beast!' she raged inwardly. 'Arrogant beast! How dare he speak to me like that? I wish I'd let him go to this wretched party on his own!'

If Monsieur Denis was aware of her unspoken resentment he gave no sign of it. They did not speak as they descended the stairs and went into the street, where a low-slung maroon saloon car was parked by the pavement.

'If I'm going to be miserable tonight at least it will be in comfort,' Lissa thought, unwillingly regaining her sense of humour, as Monsieur Denis opened the passenger door and helped her into one of the cream leather bucket seats.

The same rather strained silence persisted in the car for the first part of the journey. Lissa stole a look at her companion and was reluctantly forced to the conclusion that Jenny was right. 'He is a dish,' she thought. 'Or he would be if he could bring himself to smile occasionally. But perhaps he was very fond of the girl he was going with tonight, and he's just disappointed and I'm getting the backlash. But he didn't have to ask me, if he didn't want to. He was under no obligation at all. It can't be that. Perhaps he just doesn't like blondes. I'm sure there must be something about me personally that's annoyed him. He can't be like this with everyone, or he would have been murdered years ago. Well, someone's got to say something, so here goes.'

Trying to keep her voice light, she said, 'I believe we are going to a cocktail party, *monsieur*. May I know where?'

'At Fontaine House.'

'Fontaine Fabrics?' Lissa gasped.

'That is correct, *mademoiselle*. You know the company?'

'I've heard of it, of course, *monsieur*. Who hasn't? And of course the designs are often featured in our magazines. They're gorgeous, but I'm afraid the price puts them out of my range. Working girls and Fontaine Fabrics don't go together, I'm afraid.'

'It is true we supply mainly to couture houses,' he agreed. 'After all, if our fabrics were to be put on to the mass market, they would no longer have that exclusive quality which is their main value. However, we are not indifferent to the demands of this market, and we have certain plans, although I would have thought in many ways it was plentifully supplied already.'

He reached down and touched a fold of chiffon peeping from her velvet coat. 'This design is most charming, *par exemple*.'

'You surprise me, *monsieur*. I didn't think you had noticed.' Now why did I say that? Lissa wondered miserably, and waited to be swept by another icy blast.

'You are mistaken, *mademoiselle*. You will find that I miss very little.' His voice was almost affable, but his expression was as grim as ever.

It was almost as if he was warning her about something. But what? They were complete strangers, and if there was any justice or mercy, they would never meet again after this evening, so what could be prompting his extraordinary attitude?

And Paul? She bit back a smile. What would he make of her sardonic companion? Just shrug, probably, and order some champagne.

The car drew smoothly and noiselessly to a halt and the door was opened by a commissionaire. Lissa was helped out and conducted through wide glass doors into an enormous tiled foyer, empty but for a huge white reception desk, holding several telephones and the latest in switchboard and intercom systems. The decor was bare to the point of austerity, the plain white walls relieved only by what Lissa at first took to be very good abstract paintings, but what she realised were actually framed prints of some of Fontaines' most successful designs.

Monsieur Denis guided her past the lift, his hand firmly gripping her elbow. Lissa was acutely conscious of his touch for a reason she could not have explained even to herself.

'The party is being held on the mezzanine,' he explained. 'You do not object to climbing a few stairs?'

'Of course not.'

At the top of the short flight, a white quilted door faced them. Monsieur Denis held it open for her to pass through and they came into a gallery crowded with people. The party seemed to be in full swing, and laughter and chatter ebbed and flowed on all sides, with the chinking of glasses. Deft-footed waiters carried trays of glasses and canapés between the chattering groups of people.

'May I take your coat, madam?' A smiling woman in a black dress appeared at her elbow.

'Thank you.' Lissa undid the clasps, and was immediately aware of whose hands were slipping the coat from her shoulders. She found her pulses had quickened, and was furious with herself.

'What would you like to drink?' Monsieur Denis inquired.

'A dry sherry, please.' She forced herself into composure as a waiter hurried up in answer to his nod. He ordered her sherry and a whisky for himself, then turned back to her.

'A cigarette?' He offered her the slenderest of gold cases.

'Thank you.' Lissa opened her bag and produced her lighter. He took it from her and sent the little flame soaring with a practised flick of his thumb.

'How clever.' Lissa smiled at him, deliberately overcoming her nervousness. 'I can never get it to work for me first time.'

'The mechanism is a little stiff, I think.' He examined the lighter, black brows raised. 'A pretty toy, *très élégante*. I compliment you on your taste.'

'I am afraid the credit is due elsewhere, *monsieur*. It was a present from a friend.'

'Ah,' he said, and there was a note in that monosyllable that sent hot, indignant colour flooding her face again. At that moment the waiter returned with their drinks, and she was obliged to take hers with a murmur of thanks.

More people were arriving all the time, through a door in the centre of the gallery which Lissa guessed led to the lifts they had bypassed. She was surprised when each of the newcomers was loudly announced by a master of ceremonies, stationed at the door.

'No one announced us,' she thought. 'We came in through a side door. I hope to heaven he's not a gate-crasher or something frightful like that, but he spoke of Fontaines as if he belonged to it. It must be all right.'

She turned to look for an ash tray and a tall man, rather bald, with glasses, came hurrying towards them.

'Raoul, my dear fellow! So delighted you could make it. We don't get together nearly often enough for my liking. Why didn't you give us more warning? Helen would have laid on a dinner party. She's just looking for an excuse.'

'*Hélas*, I must return to Paris very soon.' Monsieur Denis was actually smiling at last, a genuine smile that lit up his face and made him look younger and incredibly attractive. How old was he? Lissa wondered. Early thirties, surely. He was slim for his height, but he looked wiry and he moved with a kind of whiplash grace.

There was something about him, just as Jenny had said. Only a resemblance so fleeting that she couldn't relate it at all. Probably some film star, she thought. Lissa herself rarely visited the cinema, but Jenny and Roger went regularly. In fact Jenny always declared it was Roger's resemblance to Steve McQueen which had attracted her in the first place. Again, this was a resemblance visible only to Jenny, Lissa thought amusedly.

'Mademoiselle Fairfax, may I present to you Max Prentiss, the managing director of Fontaine-London.'

As Lissa and Prentiss shook hands, Monsieur Denis continued, 'This isn't a full-scale visit, Max. I had one or two items of a personal nature to deal with. In the autumn I shall have time to spare, and to enjoy one of Hélène's excellent dinners.'

'All is forgiven, then,' Prentiss said lightly. He smiled at Lissa. 'What do you think of our latest design?'

'I haven't seen it,' Lissa glanced around. 'Is this what the party is all about?'

'My dear child,' Prentiss took her arm, 'you've been sadly neglected. What are you thinking of, Raoul? You keep this lovely creature exclusively to yourself, and you don't even show her the reason for the celebration. Shame on you! Come, my dear.'

He led Lissa along the gallery, chatting amiably and calling greetings to people as they went. A small dais had been set up halfway along the gallery, and he paused. 'There you are,' he said. 'Our latest—Bacchante.'

Lissa breathed, 'Oh!' She was looking at a cascade of material like a shimmering waterfall of green and gold, spilling endlessly on to the white carpet of the dais. Vivid splashes of colour like flames glinted here and there.

She turned to Prentiss. 'It's—fabulous. There's no other word. But surely you don't just put out one new design a season?'

'Oh, no, we are not as exclusive as that,' Prentiss smiled. 'We show the full range privately to certain invited buyers. But one is always selected to show the trend we are following in any particular range of designs.'

'I would love to see the whole range.' Lissa's eyes shone.

'I'm sure it could be arranged,' said Prentiss. 'I'll have a word with Raoul . . .'

'Oh, no, please.' Lissa flushed. 'I wouldn't dream of imposing . . .'

'Nothing of the sort,' said Prentiss. 'She wouldn't be imposing on anyone, would she, Raoul?'

Lissa realised he had come silently to stand beside them. She glanced up at him quickly and saw that he was looking amused.

'She may certainly visit the design rooms if she wishes,' he said. 'But I hope you are not suggesting Bacchante for her, though, Max. It would kill her colouring.'

'Undoubtedly,' agreed Prentiss. 'I was thinking more in terms of Midsummer Night—those deep blues, with silver undertones—against that hair, eh, Raoul?'

'*Incroyable.*' Raoul Denis drew deeply on his cigarette and Lissa was aware that he was watching her intently, and felt a blush creeping into her cheeks.

'Oh, please,' she said, laughing a little nervously. 'It's too tantalising.'

Prentiss patted her hand. 'Well, we won't tantalise you any more, but if you do come—and I hope you will—make sure you see Midsummer Night—and Venetian Glass. Just ask for me, and I'm sure you'll have no trouble getting in.'

Lissa looked at Raoul Denis inquiringly as Prentiss turned away. 'Is security so strict?'

'Of course.' He glanced around. 'There are security guards on duty now—to stop unofficial photographs mainly—but no one would guess. There have been times when our designs have been pirated. We take no chances now.'

Lissa stared at the material on the stand. 'It's quite beautiful,' she said slowly. 'It's like the whole spirit of spring—golden and glowing and innocent.'

'But with a touch of savagery underneath,' her companion agreed a little mockingly. 'Rather like a woman, wouldn't you say, *ma belle*?'

The brilliant dark eyes flickered over her, lingering on her shoulders and the slender curves revealed by the deeply cut neckline. Lissa had an overpowering urge to pull the edges of her dress together over her breasts. In spite of herself her hand went up, and brushed against the hard unfamiliar shape of Paul's brooch. It gave her an odd sense of reassurance, and she forced herself to stare back at this disconcerting stranger, who seemed so bent on tormenting her.

'Mr Prentiss is charming,' she commented, keeping her voice steady. 'Do you know all the people here?'

'No, why should I?'

Lissa felt baffled. 'Well, haven't you come here to meet anyone in particular?'

'No, it was a coincidence the design party being on this particular evening when I happened to be in London. I know the London house is being run well, so I need concern myself very little.'

Lissa could not keep sarcasm out of her voice. 'That must be a great comfort to them. What precisely do you do that makes you of such importance, *monsieur*?'

'I do very little,' he said indifferently. 'I am managing director of the French house, but that is nothing. It was my grandfather who was the important one. Fontaine was his creation, which is why our family retains the controlling interest.'

Lissa said nothing for a long moment. Then she said quietly, 'I must apologise, *monsieur*.'

'Why? You could have had no way of knowing. Apologies are unnecessary.' He glanced at his watch. 'I think we have done our duty here. It is time we were leaving for the theatre.'

Lissa would have liked another drink, several drinks in fact to nerve herself for the rest of the ordeal ahead, but instead she murmured, 'Yes,' submissively and allowed herself to be steered to the door, where her coat appeared as if by magic. She waited for a moment while Raoul Denis made his farewells, then they walked together towards the stairs.

'I have arranged for us to take a taxi to the theatre,'

Raoul Denis said.

'But why aren't we going in your car?'

'I prefer not to cope with your English parking problems. I've ordered it to meet me at your *apartement* later tonight,' he said. 'We will have dinner after the theatre.'

Lissa's heart sank. She had intended to plead a headache after the theatre, and leave him to his own devices for the rest of the evening. But it looked as if she was going to be robbed of her early night, after all.

'*Courage, ma belle.*' Was she just imagining that note of malicious amusement in his voice? 'The night is yet young.'

Eternal would be a better word, Lissa thought, as they walked through the glass doors into the coolness of the early summer evening.

# CHAPTER TWO

To Lissa's amazement, Raoul Denis seemed to under-
go a kind of sea-change as the taxi drew away from
Fontaines. He did not plague her with any more
barbed remarks as they sped through the West End,
and when he mentioned the play he had selected for
them to see, she was delighted.

'That's wonderful!' she exclaimed. 'I've been wanting to see that for ages.'

She had tried to persuade Paul to go with her on
several occasions, but he claimed that straight theatre
bored him, and he preferred the intimate cabarets in
the night clubs to which he usually took her.

It was an excellent production and the play itself
was stimulating and thought-provoking. During the
interval, Lissa found herself in the bar and realised
with a start that she and Raoul Denis had been argu-
ing for fully ten minutes about the effectiveness of the
confrontation between two of the major characters
which had led to the first act curtain. She also realised
that during this argument she had totally forgotten
how much she disliked him. She faltered with what she
was saying and looking up, found he was laughing,
and wondered uneasily if he could read her thoughts.

'Have another drink,' he said. 'Yes, we have time.
The bell hasn't gone yet. I think that little one who
plays the daughter has a future, don't you?'

Lissa, sipping her vodka and tonic, agreed.

'Do you go to the theatre much in Paris, *monsieur*?'
she asked.

'Very little, I regret,' he replied. 'Most of my spare
time is spent in the country at my house there. My

mother is to some extent an invalid, and I like to be with her as much as I can. Tell me,' he added unexpectedly, 'does your English reserve and conventionality insist on this formality, or could you not bring yourself to call me Raoul?'

Lissa nearly choked on a mouthful of her drink. It was on the tip of her tongue to remind him that the formality of the evening to date had been imposed by him, but she overcame her resentment.

'I'm not as prim and conventional as all that,' she said with a slight smile. 'I'll call you Raoul.'

'Splendid,' he approved. 'And I call you what? Lisse?'

'It's Lissa—short for Melissa, actually. My mother felt very poetic when I was born,' she said, talking nonsense to cover her embarrassment as he gave her another of his searching looks.

'And have you inspired no poetry since? I cannot believe Englishmen are so lacking in soul,' he said.

Lissa, feeling herself blushing again, was thankful when the bell rang at that moment signalling them back to their seats.

During the second act, she knew he was watching her most of the time, and she concentrated all the more fiercely on the stage. It was this scrutiny and the general oddness of his behaviour during the evening that was making her so nervous and on edge, she told herself.

As they moved through the crowded foyer after the performance, Raoul Denis asked, 'Have you any particular preference in restaurants, or are you prepared to leave the choice all to me?'

'Quite prepared,' Lissa smiled at him. 'I warn you, I enjoyed that so much that I shall expect nothing but the best.'

'*Soit.*' He sent her a swift glance. 'I trust you will

27

find the remainder of the evening even more enjoy-able.'

Again Lissa had a sense of vague unease, but as she looked inquiringly at him, he began once more to talk of the performance they had seen, and they were soon involved in a discussion which occupied the taxi ride to the quiet but very expensive restaurant he had chosen. The tables were set in alcoves round the walls, and the entire room was lit by candles, which lent an air of mystery and intimacy which immediately appealed to Lissa.

'Though it makes me feel as if I should whisper all the time,' she said, leaning back on the luxuriously upholstered bench seat.

'Why?' Raoul, sitting close beside her, sounded amused.

'Well, you can't really see who else is here,' she explained. 'It's the sort of place where people have trysts and exchange secrets.'

Raoul bent towards her until his mouth brushed her ear. 'If you have a secret to confide, *ma belle*, consider me your *confidant*.'

Lissa, disturbed by his proximity, moved hastily, and her hand caught a glass, sending it clattering across the polished table on to the thickly carpeted floor. A waiter hurried to retrieve it—luckily unbroken—and brought her another glass, while she sat, flushed and angry at her lack of poise.

He did that deliberately, she thought, but why? And she wished with all her heart that the evening was over.

As the meal proceeded, Lissa realised that Raoul Denis' knowledge of food and wines far outweighed even Paul's, whom she was used to regarding as something of an expert. The meal was delicious, and the service was swift and unobtrusive. Lissa leaned back in her seat feeling warm and relaxed, as coffee and brandy were served.

'A cigarette?' Raoul asked.

'No, thanks. It would spoil that wonderful food.' She turned to smile at him and found to her surprise that he seemed to have withdrawn to a distance. But that was idiotic. He had not moved. She closed her eyes momentarily, and when she opened them again he was watching her.

'I think the time has come for our departure,' he said softly, and signalled to the waiter.

'This is the perfect place to end an evening,' Lissa said dreamily.

'Or even to begin it,' he said, helping her to rise and putting her coat round her shoulders.

As they crossed the pavement to a waiting taxi, Lissa stumbled slightly, and Raoul's hand was instantly under her elbow.

'Take care,' he warned, and helped her into the cab.

Lissa collapsed on to the seat and again closed her eyes. The cab felt stuffy and the list of fares and regulations which faced her was oddly blurred.

'Oh, God,' she thought. 'I've had too much to drink. This is terrible!'

'Are you all right?' he asked as she pulled herself together and sat up.

'Fine,' she lied, smiling carefully. As her mind raced back, she realised she had unwittingly drunk far more than her usual modest amount—sherry before dinner and a glass of wine with a meal. There had been drinks at the party, she recalled, and the vodka at the theatre, and wine in the food at the restaurant as well as with it, not to mention that last brandy.

Coffee, she thought. Black coffee and bed as soon as possible.

Maggie would certainly look a little askance if her

secretary turned up for work the next day with an obvious hangover.

The taxi drew to a halt in front of the terraced house where the girls had their flat, and Lissa quailed at the thought of the two flights of stairs to her front door. Raoul paid off the driver and glanced up the street.

'My car does not appear to have arrived,' he remarked. 'Is there perhaps a telephone in the house?'

'Mrs Henderson doesn't have one, but there's a call box just round the corner.' Lissa hoped that she was not slurring her words. She waited for him to say goodnight and go and look for the phone box, but he showed no signs of leaving. Eventually, she felt forced to ask, 'Would you—er—like some coffee?'

'*Merci bien.*' He took the latchkey from her unresisting hand and fitted it into the lock. '*En avant!*'

Lissa was thankful to find herself at last alone in the peace and quiet of the kitchenette. Raoul had left her to make the coffee while he telephoned. She set out pottery mugs on a tray and plugged in the percolator. Her head was beginning to clear as she carried the coffee through and set it on the table in front of the gas fire.

'I lit the fire. I hope you don't mind.' Raoul Denis was standing by the table. He was holding Mrs Henderson's magazine, but as Lissa started pouring the coffee, he put it down and came to sit on the sofa.

'No, it was a good idea. It always gets chilly up here late at night, even if it is officially supposed to be early summer.' Lissa helped herself to sugar and passed the bowl to Raoul, who declined it with a slight gesture.

'Did you arrange about your car?' she asked.

'Yes, a tiresome misunderstanding. It will be here presently.'

'That's good,' she said, without thinking.

'*Je suis désolé*. Do you wish the evening to end so soon?'

'I didn't mean that,' Lissa began, leaning forward to put her mug back on the table. She was determined that he should not needle her again. Certainly he seemed very much at his ease, stretched out on the sofa.

'More coffee?' she asked.

'I thank you, but no.' He replaced his own cup. 'It was delicious, however.'

'So I've been told,' she smiled, thinking of Paul, who invariably expressed his appreciation in extravagant terms.

It was as if that smile lit a fire in Raoul.

'*Mon Dieu!*' His voice sounded suddenly hoarse, but whether it was anger or some other emotion, she could not tell. Before she had a chance to protest, he had reached for her, drawing her roughly into his arms and silencing her with his mouth.

When at last he raised his head, his eyes burned down into hers, as she lay bruised and breathless in his arms.

'*Dieu*, Lissa, do you know what you are doing to me?' he muttered. He bent to her again, but this time his mouth caressed a feverish path down her throat and searched the soft hollows between her neck and shoulders.

Lissa's pulses were pounding violently. The room swam, and she felt every nerve ending in her body throbbing insistently. Slowly her hands, which at first had been braced against his chest, crept up to clasp his neck, and her fingers twined in his hair. Murmuring endearments in his own language against her parted lips, he began to slide the chiffon from her shoulders. Her body arched towards him instinctively, welcoming his touch. His grip tightened, and the soft chiffon tore beneath his hands.

Something hard and metallic tinkled to the floor and rolled a little way. The brooch—Paul's brooch.

Lissa was suddenly, sickeningly aware of what was happening to her.

'No!' She tore herself out of his arms, catching a glimpse of herself in the mirror over the fireplace, her hair falling round her bared shoulders, her dress torn almost to the waist.

'Oh, you brute! You devil ... how dare you!'

'Dare?' He stared up at her. His eyes glittered and he looked as dangerous as a black panther. Lissa was horribly aware of her complete isolation. The couple in the flat below were on holiday and Mrs Henderson was too far away to hear any cries for help. And he knows Jenny won't be back tonight, she thought helplessly. He must have planned all this deliberately.

'I was under the impression, *ma belle,* that we had come to an understanding. Surely you are not trying to pretend that I am the first to avail myself of your— services?'

'Services?' Lissa almost choked. 'You don't mean— you can't imagine that I ... that I would let you ...'

'Until a moment ago I had every reason to think so.' His eyes went over her in insolent appraisal and she felt naked under his gaze. 'As far as I am concerned, *ma belle*, by accepting my invitation tonight, you placed yourself at my disposal. I regret that you do not see fit to keep your part of the bargain. I am still more than ready to keep mine.'

'Get out,' Lissa said between her teeth. 'Get out now before I call the police!'

'How do you propose to do that?' he asked. He laughed harshly. 'I would not be so ill-advised as to call the police if I were you. The English police are not fools, and they would know what to make of a young woman who allows a man to wine and dine her for the evening and then calls "Rape" in her *apartement*. Besides, you are unharmed, except perhaps for your dress—and your pride.'

He picked up his light overcoat from a chair and walked to the door.

'*Bonne nuit,*' he said, with a slight bow, and was gone.

Lissa rushed to the door and locked it, then leaned her forehead against the cool white-painted panels, listening to his footsteps going downstairs. Her breath came in great shuddering sobs, and she shivered violently.

Eventually, as her self-control returned, she walked slowly to the bedroom and threw herself across her bed. She felt numbed, yet her throat ached fiercely and her eyes pricked with tears.

Bitterly she blamed herself for agreeing to go out with him in the first place. Yet Paul knew him and obviously trusted him.

The most shaming part was that she herself had allowed it. She had made no effort to resist—had not even wanted to resist, until the memory of Paul had been forced back into her mind, almost by accident.

Paul! If he knew! She shuddered and buried her face in the ivory-coloured quilt. Would the Denis man tell him? Somehow she doubted it. But he must never find out. He would be incredibly hurt, and rightly so, that she could behave like that with a man who was not only a stranger, but whose whole manner from the beginning had betrayed a strange kind of contempt for her.

The worst of it was that she was still conscious of him. It was as if the pressure of his lips and hands was a lesson that once learned, she could never forget. She sat up slowly, raking the silky mass of pale hair back from her face, her eyes brooding. She looked down at her torn dress with revulsion, then jerking at the fastenings, stripped it off and flung it to the floor. She would throw it away and make some excuse for its disappearance. It had been her favourite, but now the sight of it was unbearable.

It was chilly in the bedroom, and she put on her black and silver housecoat before wandering restlessly back into the warmth of the living room. She looked round, wishing with all her might that Jenny was not staying the night with Roger and his parents. Normally Lissa had no objection to being on her own, but now she desperately needed to hear a friendly voice, and not have to sit alone with her thoughts.

A hot drink of milk and a couple of aspirins. That was the answer—and some noise. She picked up the transistor radio, twisting the controls until she found some quiet, rather sentimental music, and carried it into the kitchen with her while she heated her milk.

She returned to the living room and set the milk down on the coffee table, still littered with the cups she had used for coffee with Raoul. Then she went over to the sideboard for the aspirin. Her eye was caught by a message on the pad there in Jenny's writing. 'Maggie popped in just after you went, full of beans, full of mystery too. Something wonderful has happened, but she's going to tell you herself tomorrow. Be good. Love. J.'

Lissa frowned a little. This was getting to be a night for mysteries and she would welcome a little plain speaking from now on. She put the pad down and picked up Mrs Henderson's magazine.

It might not be the most stimulating reading in the world, but that was all the better if it helped her put the evening's events out of her mind and helped her get to sleep. As she sat down on the sofa with it, it fell open on her lap, and she saw a corner of one of the pages had been deliberately turned down. Not only that, but someone, presumably Mrs Henderson, had carefully outlined one of the pictures on the page in blue ballpoint pen.

'What in the world...?' Lissa looked down unbelievingly. The occasion that was being reported was a dance at the French Embassy some weeks ago when she had first started going out with Paul. And there they both were, standing together at the foot of a staircase, quite oblivious of the fact that they were being photographed. There was a paragraph about them too, referring to Paul as a 'playboy diplomat' and describing Lissa as 'his latest girl about town'.

As if she was something rather nasty in the City, Lissa thought, her sense of humour reasserting itself. So this was what Mrs Henderson meant by her cryptic note! How awful, she thought, hoping that no one else she knew had seen it.

Her thoughts stopped there with a vivid memory of searing anger in a man's eyes, and the magazine being thrown down contemptuously.

That must have been what made him so angry, Lissa realised, but it certainly did not explain why it affected him like that.

It was beyond her, she decided, as she drank the last of her milk. She could only be thankful that she would never have to see that Denis man again as long as she lived. And if Paul mentioned him, she would just have to change the subject.

But the thought brought her surprisingly little comfort, either then or in the long hours that followed before she finally drifted into an uneasy sleep.

Lissa did not feel particularly refreshed when the buzzing of the alarm brought her unwillingly back to wakefulness the next morning. As she sat up to switch it off, she sniffed experimentally. There was an unmistakable odour of coffee, and even as she threw the covers to go and investigate, the bedroom door opened and Jenny walked in smiling with two cups on a tray. It was then for the first time that Lissa realised that the other bed was crumpled.

'So you didn't stay at Roger's after all?' she exclaimed.

'No, his mother wasn't feeling too well—some virus thing, I think, so he brought me back here late. You were dead to the world. By the way, you owe me thanks for doing the washing up.'

'Washing up?' Lissa stared at her, puzzled, then remembered, crimsoning, last night's debris still left in the living room.

'And you'd left the gas fire on,' Jenny said reprovingly. 'Whatever was the matter? Surely the Pirate King didn't have that much effect on you?'

Lissa sipped her coffee, trying to avoid Jenny's gaze, but it was no use. Jenny came and sat on the edge of the bed, and gave her a long, even stare.

'Come on, tell me all about it. Was it lucky or unlucky that I returned last night?'

Lissa put the cup down on the small chest of drawers that separated the twin beds, and her lips trembled.

'Oh, Jen,' she mumbled, 'it was awful!' And in brief, staccato phrases she outlined the events of the evening, leading up to his attempted seduction.

Jenny sat open-mouthed with astonishment. 'But he was a friend of Paul's! He brought that note. What kind of a man is he to behave like that to his friend's girl?'

'He didn't actually say they were friends, but old acquaintances,' Lissa said miserably. 'Perhaps he dislikes Paul and was trying to do something to hurt him.'

'Are you going to say anything to Paul?'

'Oh, no!' Lissa gave a quick shiver. 'What could I say? That ... creature was right—he could have had me. He nearly did, if it hadn't been for that brooch. Oh, heavens, I've just remembered! It fell off, and I've probably lost it. He probably took it with him for spite. Oh, Jenny, what am I going to do?'

'Drink the rest of that coffee before it gets cold,' said Jenny calmly. 'And stop worrying about the family heirloom. I found it on the rug. I just avoided stepping on it, and it's safe and sound back in its little velvet box. I was right, you see, to persuade you to wear it. Otherwise think what I might have found when I walked in ...' She sighed and cast a pious look at the ceiling, and Lissa gave an unwilling chuckle.

'Jenny,' she said, after a slight pause, 'how do you feel with Roger?'

Jenny put down her cup and gave her a straight look. 'You mean when we're kissing, and making love and all that?'

'Yes.' Lissa drank some more coffee. 'It's an awful cheek asking you, I know, but I can't judge what I should feel with Paul. I thought everything was perfect—but last night ...' she paused and the colour came into her cheeks. 'I didn't know anyone could feel like that.'

'Men like Raoul Denis should either be locked up securely, or be made more readily available to us all,' Jenny said, grinning. She took Lissa's hand. 'I can't tell you about Roger and me, because it wouldn't mean anything. All I can say is that when you meet the right man, you'll know. There won't be any doubts. But don't be deceived by some Continental Romeo who's probably had more women than we've had hot dinners. That's not love. Passion is a thing apart. Don't mix the two until you're sure of the first one.'

Lissa sighed. 'I'm not sure of anything any more. Thank you for rescuing the brooch. I shall feel worse than ever about returning it now. What am I going to say to him?'

'What you planned to say last night before the Pirate King took all the wind out of your sails. That it's too expensive a gift at this stage in your relationship, and that you have to get to know him much better before you can even consider marriage.' Jenny cast her eyes to heaven. 'Would you like me to come along as prompter?'

Lissa laughed. 'No, I think I'll manage the words once the action starts. Now I'd better start getting dressed or I shall be late.'

She even managed a second cup of coffee and a slice of toast before, dressed in a light cream woollen dress with a matching coat, she set off for the underground. She felt more cheerful when she arrived at Maggie's flat. Her godmother had been left a wealthy widow some years before, but even so she earned a more than adequate income from her very popular books. She was a tall woman with naturally waving grey hair, and still very attractive although well into her fifties. Lissa adored her, but often felt she could not have been the easiest person in the world to live with when her husband was alive.

Maggie, when she was engaged on a novel, had a habit of spending most of the night covering sheet upon sheet of paper in her small neat handwriting for Lissa to transcribe the following day. Trim in a bright red jersey suit, she swung round from her desk as Lissa entered. 'My dear, thank goodness you've come at last!'

'I'm not late, am I?' Lissa asked, puzzled, and glanced at her watch.

'No, of course not. Didn't Jenny give you my message?'

'Why, yes, she left it on the pad. What's all the mystery?'

'Firstly, is your passport in order?'

'Yes.' Lissa stared at her. 'What on earth . . .?'

'Not what, ducky, but where,' said Maggie triumphantly. 'How would you like to spend the next month or so staying in a French chateau that was actually looted at the time of the Revolution, and was only saved from being burned to the ground by a few loyal peasants?' She got up smiling. 'And that's not all. Many of the papers relating to that time have been preserved very carefully, including a diary kept by the old Comte—until they marched him off to be guillotined. And we've been invited to make what use we like of all this material.'

'Oh, Maggie!' Lissa's eyes sparkled. 'It's like a dream. What could be better? How did it happen?'

'Aha!' Maggie waved her finger. 'The old Comte lost his head, but his son kept his and got away to England with most of the family jewels intact. He married a wealthy English heiress and when things returned to normal in France he went back and restored the chateau, and had a son, who had another son . . .'

'I suppose this family tree is leading somewhere,' Lissa said, grinning.

'Indeed it is, ducky. To one Monsieur Paul de Gue, whom we have to thank for this invitation. Darling boy! It was like a bolt from the blue.'

'Paul owns a chateau?' Lissa said incredulously.

'Well, his elder brother, who is the present Comte de Gue, actually owns it, but of course it's Paul's home too. His mother lives there and Paul apparently wrote to her when he heard I was planning a book about the time of the Reign of Terror and suggested his great-great-grandpapa's romantic adventures could make a marvellous book—and she agreed. I've had the most charming letter from her, endorsed by the Comte himself. Well, what is it, dear? I thought you'd be delighted.'

'I am delighted—for you,' Lissa said with a forced smile. 'It's just that . . . do I have to go as well?'

'Of course. You're my secretary. I couldn't possibly manage without you. You're used to my ways and you know how that beastly typewriter sticks or unravels its ribbon all over me every time I go near it. Besides, I thought that you and Paul—well, it seemed ideal.'

'That's the trouble.' Lissa moved to the desk and began to straighten some of the papers that littered it. 'It's too ideal. I expect you'll think I'm mad like Jenny does, but I haven't made up my mind yet about Paul. I don't know whether it will work. It rather seems as if this invitation is just more pressure on me to say yes.'

'On the other hand, seeing him on his own ground and against the rest of the family might make up your mind for you. People are more themselves in their own homes. You might like him better with some of the foreign diplomat glamour knocked off him,' Maggie said surprisingly.

'I thought you liked him.'

'I do. I think he's a charming boy, but his biggest trouble is that he thinks so too.'

Lissa smiled a little wanly. 'Perhaps you're right, and after all, he won't be there all the time. He has his work to do.'

'I wouldn't count on that keeping him away. He mentioned to me recently that he had some leave due. I think he intends to be guide, philosopher and friend on this visit.' Maggie gave her a shrewd glance. 'It's getting you down, isn't it? You have a peaky look. A few weeks abroad will do you the world of good, whether the handsome Paul is in attendance or not.'

'Yes,' Lissa sighed. 'Oh, Maggie, why can't life be simple and spelled out in black and white for us?'

'Because it would be no fun if it were—and talking about spelling things out, why don't you pop the coffee on while I try and sort some of last night's stuff out for you?'

Maggie had spent a long and fruitful night, and Lissa typed steadily until noon. She had paused for a cigarette when the phone by her elbow rang. She picked up the receiver and gave the number.

'*Chérie*!'

'Oh, Paul, it's good to hear from you!'

'I am afraid you won't be so pleased when I tell you what I have to say. I must postpone our date for this evening—something has come up. I am ringing to see if you are free for lunch instead. The little Italian place in—say, half an hour.'

'That'll be fine.' Lissa tried to mask her disappointment.

'*Au revoir*, then.'

Lissa replaced the receiver and finished typing the sheet she was engaged on. It was the second time Paul had broken a date with her, and she felt oddly disconcerted.

'How funny,' she thought wryly, 'if all the time I'm wondering if I want to marry him, he's wondering exactly the same about me.'

Paul was at the restaurant when she arrived.

'I've ordered dry martinis. I hope that's what you wanted,' he said, helping her off with her coat.

'Perfect,' she assured him. A waiter arrived for their

order and they spent a few minutes wrangling amicably over the respective merits of ravioli and lasagne.

'Not that it really matters,' Lissa said when the waiter finally disappeared with his order. 'All the food here tastes marvellous.'

'*C'est vrai*. This is one of the places I shall miss most when I leave.'

'You're leaving London?' Lissa stared at him.

'Within a week or so.' He laid his hand on hers. 'But you see how I arrange things. I must return home, so I pull strings and my Lissa comes with me.'

'I wondered what lay behind this sudden passion for historical research of yours,' Lissa said drily.

'Do you blame me? Ah, I think you do a little. But think, *chérie*, I want you to see my home—the estate—and meet my family. I had hoped it would be as my fiancée, but I accept what you say, and will wait patiently for you. Maman knows nothing except that Madame Desmond, whose books she so greatly admires, is to stay with us and that her secretary will be with her. She is happy. Madame Desmond is happy, because she will have the chateau to look over—and the papers. I am happy, so why should not you be a little happy too?'

Lissa laughed. 'I'll try and be a little happy, although actually I feel shattered,' she confessed. 'I had no idea you lived in a chateau. Has it got turrets and dungeons?'

'A few,' Paul said airily. 'Much of the original building was destroyed at the time of the Revolution, you understand, and when Henri de Gue returned to France he decided he'd had enough of the style of the *ancien régime*, and so had the peasants, so he rebuilt the living quarters in a style he considered modern.'

'A man of diplomacy,' Lissa smiled. 'Are you like him? Is this why you entered the Diplomatic Service?'

'*Non*,' Paul shrugged. 'One has to do something, and the family business did not interest me.'

He broke off as the waiter arrived with the meal. When they were served and the wine was poured, he went on, 'Anyway, that is all over now. It has been decided that I am to return to St Denis and learn how to manage the estate. Jacques Tarrand is growing old, and his only son was killed in Algeria during his military service.'

'Will you like managing the estate?' Lissa sipped her wine.

'It will be better than being an office boy at the Embassy,' he said, and Lissa felt a touch of compunction at the way she had criticised him to Jenny for his attitude to his work.

'Perhaps this will steady him and give him a sense of purpose,' she thought. 'He really is very sweet, but so young for his age.'

As they ate, Paul told her a little about the chateau, high on a wooded hill outside the village, which was situated on the banks of a small river.

Lissa wanted to ask about his family, but decided not to press the point when he did not volunteer any information. After all, she thought, she would be meeting them soon, and would be able to draw her own conclusions.

It was the thought of his family that brought the memory of the brooch to mind, and she hunted in her handbag for the flat velvet case.

'Paul, please don't be angry, but I can't accept this from you. It's a lovely present, but it's too valuable to give me as things stand at present. If ever we come to—an agreement I'd be proud to wear it, but for the time being I think it would be best if you kept it.'

Paul's fingers closed over hers as she handed him the case. 'My lovely Lissa,' he said. 'You are the only girl I

43

can think of who would have done that. You are very strong-minded, *chérie*. Many women would have kept the brooch, I think.'

Lissa's eyes were stormy. 'I am not many women,' she retorted. 'Are you in the habit of handing out expensive gifts like that to every girl you come across?'

'*Mais non*,' Paul smiled placatingly at her. 'That was a very special gift, only for you, my Lissa. The brooch is very old. It is among the jewels that Comte Henri took with him when he fled the *sans-culottes*, and it is always given as a betrothal gift to the bride of the second son ... what is it, *chérie*, are you ill?'

'No,' Lissa gulped down some wine, and the colour began to return to her cheeks. 'Paul, that was unforgivable of you. You should have told me what the brooch was—its significance. You must have known I would never have taken it at all if I had the remotest idea ...'

'*Précisément*, and that's why I didn't tell you. I'm sorry, *chérie*.' Paul looked like a scolded child for all his sophistication and self-assurance. 'As soon as I made up my mind I wanted you for my wife I wrote to Maman and asked her to send me the brooch. It arrived after you had told me that you wanted more time to consider, and I could hardly send it back without some explanation.'

'Oh, no,' Lissa said bitterly. 'That would have meant a loss of face. I quite understand.'

'You are angry with me.' He stroked her cheek caressingly. 'Don't be angry with me, *ma petite*. What fault have I committed but wanting you too much?'

Lissa gave him a level look. 'I meant every word I said, Paul. And when I come to the chateau, it will be as Maggie's secretary, no more. I'll have to trust you not to make life too difficult for me.'

'Difficult?' Paul grinned at her disarmingly. 'When you come to the chateau, my Lisse, the sun will shine for you and a million roses will thrill the air with their beauty. I tell you now—you will never want to leave.'

# CHAPTER THREE

A WHIRLWIND three weeks later, Lissa and Maggie were clutching each other's hands and laughing nervously as the plane circled above Le Bourget where Paul was to meet them.

'Flying would be heaven, if it wasn't for the going up and down,' Maggie remarked as the aircraft taxied to a halt.

'Amen to that,' Lissa said devoutly. 'Look, I can see Paul. He's waving to us.'

Paul was suntanned and smiling when, the customs and passport formalities at an end, he greeted them and helped to stow their luggage into a cream Citroën estate car.

'New?' Lissa ran her hand appreciatively over the immaculate bodywork.

'*Oui*.' Paul gave a petulant shrug. 'I preferred my other car, but this is supposed to be more useful for my job.'

Lissa glanced at him a little anxiously. This was part of Paul's spoiled child act, and not the most pleasing side of his character, although it was rarely seen. Usually his behaviour in front of Maggie was perfect, but on the whole Lissa decided it might not be a bad idea if her godmother got a more balanced view of his nature.

As the journey progressed, however, Paul became more cheerful, and by the time they stopped for lunch at a small *auberge* where the tables were set outside under a striped awning in the warm sunlight, the atmosphere was as light-hearted as Lissa could have wished for her first visit to France.

She was aware too of admiring glances from some of the men already seated at adjoining tables. One of them was quietly strumming on an accordion, and Paul and Maggie roared with laughter at Lissa's embarrassment when he suddenly struck up *'Auprès de ma blonde'* with everyone joining in the chorus.

They ate some excellent home-made paté, followed by a fricassée of chicken and mushrooms and toasted the success of the new book in *vin ordinaire*.

'Bless you both,' Maggie smiled at them. 'I think we really ought to drink a toast to your brother, Paul—to Monsieur le Comte de Gue, who has kindly given us the freedom of his home.'

They drank, but Lissa was disturbed to see Paul's geniality give way to a sudden scowl, while he only perfunctorily raised his glass to his lips. Was it his brother, she wondered, who had made him get rid of the low-slung Italian sports car which had been his pride and joy, and replace it with the 'more useful' estate?

'There's obviously been trouble of some kind,' she decided ruefully to herself. 'I just hope it's all blown over by the time we get there.'

Maggie was easygoing herself and needed a congenial atmosphere to work in. It would be disastrous as well as embarrassing if their stay at the chateau was to be punctuated by family rows.

They drove on steadily towards St Denis, through rolling wooded country, the car windows down, revelling in the mellow warmth of the day.

'We will be there before tea,' Paul told them. 'Oh, yes, we keep up the English custom, although Madame Grand'mère no longer lives with us. She prefers the climate at Antibes.'

'Your grandmother is English?' Lissa asked.

*'Vraiment.'* He threw her a quick smile. 'It is a

family tradition for de Gues to marry English wives. A tradition I hope to follow,' he added in a much lower voice.

So much, Lissa thought, for all his promises to treat her simply as Maggie's secretary, nothing more nor less, for the duration of her stay. She was aware that Maggie was smiling indulgently and tried to present a façade of indifference.

Maggie dozed for a while as the car sped on and Lissa felt herself getting drowsy after the excellent meal, but she fought her sleepiness away when Paul told her that St Denis was only two kilometres away.

'We go down now into the valley,' he explained. 'One can hardly see the chateau from the village because of the trees, but I will stop at the bridge where there is a view.'

St Denis was a delightful village, with narrow streets, and tall houses, their stonework washed in pastel colours. There was a small market in the town square, which was ringed by plane trees, and Paul's car was instantly recognised and became the focus for good-natured attention. Paul drove slowly, keeping a careful eye on the throng of people, children and animals, and giving smiling waves to the many greetings that came his way.

'Now I know how royalty feels,' Lissa said as the car threaded its way out of the square and through another narrow street. They turned a corner and the river was before them—a placid rather shallow affair spanned by a sturdy stone bridge. Paul parked a little way from it, and helped Lissa from the car.

'*Allons*,' he commanded, and led her on to the bridge. Before her the road curved upwards into a dark mass of trees. Lissa followed his pointing finger and caught a glimpse of grey towers rearing above the massed trunks. She was filled with a strange breathless excitement. It was like all the fairy tales she had ever known—with the castle crouching almost unseen among the clustering trees—a place where one might find the Sleeping Beauty, or even Bluebeard, who had been the Frenchman Gilles de Rais, Lissa recalled with some amusement.

She turned to Paul. 'It's out of this world! I can't wait to see it close at hand.'

'We had better go. My mother becomes anxious if I am even a minute later than she thinks I should be,' Paul said. His affectionate tone and the smile that accompanied the words gave Lissa a slant for the first time on Paul's regard for his mother. She had been feeling a little nervous about meeting such a formidable lady as a French countess, even on formal business terms, without the added anxiety of her tenuous relationship with Paul. Now the Comtesse de Gué suddenly seemed alive, and real—a person of emotions and affections rather than simply blue blood and tradition.

The road ran along beside a high grey wall for some distance before the great arched gateway came into view. Paul swung the car under the archway and drove round the broad gravelled sweep of drive enclosing formal flowerbeds, statuary and even fountains which led to the stone steps up to the main door of the building. The steps were flanked on each side by a wide terrace with a balustrade fronting long windows which, Lissa supposed, led to the main rooms. How lovely, she thought, to be able to step through the open windows on to the terrace on warm nights. As she looked, she noticed that someone—a girl in a white dress—had done precisely that and was standing looking down at them. She appeared to be watching their arrival intently, but she made no attempt to wave or attract their attention.

'*Viens, chérie.* You are day-dreaming.' Paul sounded amused. 'Madame Barrat is waiting to greet us.'

Lissa saw a plump white-haired woman in a dark dress standing smiling at the top of the steps.

'Is she the housekeeper?' she asked. Madame Barrat looked altogether too homely and welcoming against her splendid background to be any kind of chatelaine.

'She is that, and more,' said Paul. 'She came to the chateau when my father was a child. Sometimes when my brother and I were little and had been punished for some crime, she would give us bonbons and tell us of Papa and his misdeeds when he too was small.' He laughed. 'How we loved her for that!'

Madame Barrat greeted them warmly, and told them that Madame la Comtesse awaited them in the *petit salon.*

'Is my mother alone, Thérèse?' Paul asked causally, slipping an arm around Madame's waist as they entered the large stone-flagged hall with its sweeping staircase leading to long galleries above. Lissa tried to absorb as much as possible of her surroundings without staring too obviously.

'Paul, it's enchanting,' Maggie declared, gazing round in sheer delight. 'If I can't give these puppets in my head flesh and blood while I'm here, then I don't deserve to write another line.' She glanced at some of the pictures. 'Are those family portraits?'

'A few of them,' said Paul. 'Our most valuable pictures and other heirlooms are kept in a special gallery on the first floor. I shall show it to you myself first thing tomorrow.'

Madame Barrat paused before one of the doors.

'But Madame Desmond is to see the gallery tonight, Monsieur Paul,' she said. 'When Monsieur le Comte arrived from Paris this morning he ordered that the gallery heating should be switched on before dinner.'

'My brother is here?' Paul's tone was furious.

'*Certainement*,' Madame Barrat returned placidly. 'And he too has brought a guest.'

She threw open the door and ushered them into a room attractively furnished with sofas and chairs covered in brocades in muted colours. A woman was sitting in a high-backed chair by a small fire blazing in the heart, and she immediately rose as they entered. Paul stepped forward, and carried her outstretched hands to his lips before kissing her cheek. She was a tall woman, still slender, with a lively if not conventionally pretty face. Her grey hair, blue-rinsed, was drawn back from her face into a smooth bun, and she wore an exquisitely cut dress in hyacinth blue.

Paul performed the introductions with his usual aplomb, but Lissa saw that a trace of the sullenness encountered earlier in the day had returned. She was relieved that he introduced her to his mother simply as Mademoiselle Fairfax.

'If everyone is being introduced, I suppose I had better present myself.' The drawled remark came from the window. A girl was standing there, framed by sunlight. She was small and dark, and wore a sleeveless white dress, impeccably cut, highlighted only by a gold brooch at the high neckline. She was the one who was watching us just now, Lissa realised.

She looked pretty and expensive and well-groomed, and Lissa, under her scrutiny, felt that her clothes were creased by the journey and that her make-up needed a complete overhaul.

'Dominique!' Paul sounded completely astonished. 'What are you doing here?'

The girl smiled at him, pouting a little.

'You don't sound very pleased to see me, *chéri*. Your brother invited me for a visit, and *naturellement* when I heard he was also to have as his guest Madame

Desmond, the famous novelist—I could not refuse.'

There was nothing in the words themselves to give offence, and yet Lissa knew instantly that Dominique had never heard of Maggie before that afternoon, and would have survived without difficulty if destiny had decreed that they never met. She glanced at Maggie and saw her smiling easily and putting out her hand.

'It's always nice to meet one of my fans,' she said. 'Won't you introduce me to your friend, Paul dear?'.

Bravo, Maggie, Lissa thought silently. Lesson One in manners for Mademoiselle, and long overdue by the sound of it.

The newcomer was introduced to them both as Dominique Vaumont by a tight-lipped Paul. Lissa wondered if the girl, who had come as the guest of the Comte, was the future Comtesse, although her small hands were ringless. She certainly seemed very much in charge of the situation, and when Madame de Gue drew Maggie over to one of the sofas to begin a low-voiced conversation, Dominique lost no time in twining her slim arm through Paul's.

'*Viens, chéri*,' she said, not sparing Lissa a second glance. 'Take me on to the terrace and tell me all your news from London. Your letters were not exactly—illuminating.'

Paul freed himself with a certain abruptness.

'I think tea is coming. I regret that our stroll must be postponed,' he observed. 'Anyway, Dominique, I don't think my activities in London would be of great interest to you.'

Dominique smiled up at him, deliberately provocative, her eyes glinting through her heavily mascaraed lashes.

'Oh, but you are wrong, *chéri*,' she murmured. 'I find all that you do of an overwhelming fascination, believe me.'

Paul was saved from replying as the door behind him opened and two maids wheeled in trolleys laden with china and plates of pastries under the smiling supervision of Madame Barrat.

To Lissa, she murmured, 'Real English tea, *ma petite*, so do not fear. That will be good after your journey, *hein*? And the water has been boiled as Madame la Grand'mère of the Comte taught me well.'

Soon Lissa found herself ensconced on another sofa, a steaming cup on a small table beside her and a plate with a delicious concoction of chocolate, flaked almonds and cream tempting her to forget completely the diet that she and Jenny had sometimes remembered to follow in London.

Madame de Gue, seated opposite, leaned forward and addressed her kindly.

'I understand, *mademoiselle*, that you are not simply Madame's secretary, but also her goddaughter.'

'That is so, *madame*.' Lissa was uncomfortably aware that Dominique, sitting nearby, having curtly declined anything to eat and drink, was studying her from head to foot.

'Ah, what a consolation to your parents,' Madame turned to Maggie. 'It is such a worry when these young girls leave home for the city. My own daughter Anne-Marie is just such a one. She works for a fashion magazine in Paris. Fortunately she shares an *apartement* with the daughter of my cousin, in whom I repose much confidence. Nevertheless I am very often anxious.'

She gave Lissa another charming smile before recommencing her conversation with Maggie.

Lissa, reaching for her cup, encountered a long, speculative stare from Dominique and to her annoyance found herself flushing a little. Paul, who had been standing by the window, apparently deep in

53

thought, crossed the room and sat down beside her.

'When tea is over, come for a walk with me,' he invited. 'I want to show you the gardens.'

'Oh, Paul,' his mother broke in, her brows raised.
'*La pauvre*! She has not seen her room yet, or been
able to rest from her journey. There are weeks ahead
to show Mademoiselle all these things. Do not exhaust
her on her first day with us.'

Lissa smiled gratefully. 'I am a little tired,' she
acknowledged. 'Do you mind very much, Paul?'

'Of course it is for you to decide,' he replied, but
Lissa saw that again he was scowling a little. Some of
her excitement and pleasure was beginning to evapor-
ate, as anxiety returned. She had never seen Paul quite
so moody before. He had obviously been annoyed to
find his brother had arrived before him, and yet the
Comte de Gue had more right than anyone to come
and go as he pleased in his own home.

She began to wonder what he was like, but did not
care to ask Paul. And just where did Dominique fit
into the picture? Lissa decided she had been wrong to
put her down as the Comte's future wife. For one thing
her attitude to Paul seemed pointed, to say the least,
and Lissa felt too that Madame de Gue would have
made some special mention of the fact if Dominique
were to be the future mistress of the chateau.

She felt wretched about the ambiguity of her own
position and wished that she had settled matters with
Paul one way or the other before leaving England. At
present, she occupied a kind of no-man's-land, and it
was an uncomfortable sensation. She did not know
whether her attitude towards Dominique went as far
as jealousy, but she wouldn't have been human not to
have been annoyed at the other girl's proprietorial
manner towards Paul. Surely she wouldn't be as pos-
sessive as that without encouragement, she thought,

and it also seems as if he's been writing to her. Lissa wondered if Paul would have mentioned Dominique to her if she had agreed to an official engagement back in London.

Tea was ending, and Madame de Gue rang the bell to summon Madame Barrat to show Lissa and Maggie to their rooms.

Lissa felt an almost physical relief as the door swung shut between herself and Dominique, and she adjured herself to get a grip on herself as they followed Madame's comfortable figure across the hall and up the stairs. She's probably the type who regards other women as competition even when there aren't any men around, Lissa thought, recalling the whole seductive performance they had just witnessed.

They turned left along the gallery and then moved through an arched doorway with a midnight blue velvet curtain looped back from it with a gold tas-selled cord, along a lengthy corridor, carpeted in the same colour, with doors on each side. Madame con-ducted them up another staircase which branched to the right along yet another corridor and paused before a door halfway along it.

'This is your room, Madame Desmond. The maid who will wait on you is Mathilde and she has un-packed for you. Mademoiselle Fairfax is next door to you, and the bathroom separates your rooms. I hope you have all you need, but please ring me if there is anything lacking.'

Lissa could not resist an exclamation of sheer delight when she saw her room. The dominant feature was the bed—a small fourposter, with a white lace canopy and bedspread. The curtains at the windows too were white, but the fitted carpet was a deep pink—a colour repeated in a paler shade in the silky wallpaper.

When she was alone, she walked across to the window and stood looking down into a small walled garden, a riot of early summer flowers. She stretched her arms above her head and stood sensuously revelling in the warmth of the sun. Then she took off her light navy jersey travelling suit and the high-necked white silk blouse she wore with it, and put on her housecoat which she found hanging with the rest of her clothes in the fitted white wardrobes with louvred doors which ran the length of one wall.

The bathroom was the last word in turquoise and gold tiled luxury, with a white fluffy carpet underfoot. Lissa knocked at Maggie's door.

'Is it all right if I have a bath?' she called.

'Fine,' Maggie sounded sleepy. 'I'll have mine later. I feel like a doze now.'

Lissa found that the hot scented soak dissolved much of the tiredness and cramp from her limbs. She too had intended to rest for a while before dinner, but she felt so refreshed that she changed into a pair of purple corded slacks and a thin black wool sweater and decided to go in search of the little garden she had seen from her window. She hoped rather guiltily that she would not run into Paul, after pleading her fatigue earlier.

She thought she could remember the way downstairs, but when she eventually reached the ground floor she realised she had taken a wrong turning and was in a part of the chateau well away from the family living quarters. She could hear voices in the distance, and the delectable odours drifting her way told her that she must be near the kitchen area. She went along a narrow stone-flagged passage and pulled open a heavy door at the end of it, to find herself facing a square sunny courtyard with cobbled stones underfoot. There were loose boxes on two sides, and some of them were occupied.

The walled garden was forgotten. Lissa had ridden regularly as a child and she still occasionally hired a horse in London at the weekends. She began to walk around the stable yards reading the names above the boxes.

'Mistral,' she said softly, pausing before one stall. The handsome bay who had watched her approach thrust his head towards her, his velvet muzzle questing her caressing fingers for titbits.

'I've nothing for you, love,' Lissa ran her hand up the smooth neck. 'I'll bring something next time— sugar, eh, or carrots. At least I know where the kitchens are—I think.'

The horses in the other boxes were disturbed by her presence and moving about, and the noise they made hid the sound of booted footsteps on the cobbles. It did not, however, mask the softly spoken *'Diable!'* in a voice that Lissa had never expected or wanted to hear again as long as she lived.

She whirled round with a gasp to come face to face with Raoul Denis, standing only a few feet away, his dark face rigid with incredulity and anger.

# CHAPTER FOUR

HE was the first to break the silence that seemed to stretch eternally between them.

'So, *mademoiselle*,' he said coldly. 'You have had the actual audacity to present yourself at this house.'

'The audacity is yours, *monsieur*.' The initial shock at seeing him was wearing off and Lissa felt her temper rising. 'I am here at the invitation of the Comte de Gue himself, whatever the explanation of your presence may be.'

'Indeed?' he said. 'And have you had the opportunity yet to meet your host?' There was a sarcastic inflection on the last word and Lissa realised furiously that he did not believe her. She made an effort to control herself.

'Not yet,' she acknowledged. 'As a matter of fact, I understand his being here is rather unexpected...'

'Certainly, as far as you are concerned,' he said bitingly.

'No,' Lissa fought to keep her temper. 'Frankly, *monsieur*, I'm beginning to regret that I ever set eyes on this house or any of the people in it!'

'Then that is easily remedied.' His voice was ice. 'I will arrange at once for a car to take you back to Paris. No doubt you are capable of returning to London from there without further assistance.'

'How dare you!' Lissa was almost beside herself. 'You—you have no right to behave like this.'

'I have every right,' he said. 'If, as you claim, I extended an invitation to you to visit this house, then surely I may equally withdraw it, if I wish.'

'You invited me?' Lissa stared at him open-mouthed. 'Are you trying to say—that you...' She paused helplessly, unable to credit the unpalatable truth which his words had brought home.

'Indeed yes, *mademoiselle*.' He made a slight bow. 'As you seem to have guessed at last, I am your unwitting host, Raoul de St Denis, Comte de Gue.'

Lissa felt physically sick. How could she have been so blind, so crassly stupid not to have known? The resemblance to someone they knew that Jenny had remarked on—how could she not have seen that it was Paul the stranger resembled, although Paul was much the fairer of the two.

Fighting emotions that threatened to overwhelm her in a flood of humiliated tears, she lifted her chin and looked at him.

'I see—now,' she said. 'May I ask the reason for your masquerade in London?'

'The answer is obvious, I should think,' he said.

'Not to me.'

'*Eh bien*? Then I will explain. It was, shall we say, brought to my attention that my young fool of a brother was infatuated with a young woman of whom very little was known. Soon there were pictures and journals containing items of gossip, that did little to reassure me. You were a "girl about town", I believe, and it was indicated that my brother was far from being the only man in your life. It was made clear, *mademoiselle*, that you were a member of your London "permissive society", to say the least, willing to go out with any man with sufficient money to pay for your pleasures. Wait, *s'il vous plaît*.' He held up his hand as Lissa was about to interrupt hotly. 'At that time I was prepared to let your *affaire* with my brother run its course. We have all been young and foolish in our time, *bien entendu*, but it seemed in this case you were holding out for higher stakes than usual—marriage, no less.' He paused and his eyes raked her slim figure.

'This,' he added slowly, 'I could not allow, so I decided to intervene personally. It was time, I felt, for Paul to abandon his flirtation with the Diplomatic Service too and begin some serious work on the estate here for the first time in his life.'

Lissa's heart was pounding so violently that she felt as if she would choke with the tumult inside her.

'I see,' she got out with difficulty. 'But having arranged for Paul to be removed from my apparently evil influence, couldn't you have been satisfied? Was there any reason to deceive me in that abominable way—to insult me?'

'I must confess to a certain curiosity,' he said. 'I had no real plan for the evening, and Paul of course never intended that I should deliver his note to you. I acquired it so that I could meet you and satisfy my judgement of you. But what happened was dictated as soon as you opened the door. I saw you were wearing the brooch...'

'The brooch?' Lissa repeated mechanically.

'Yes, *mademoiselle*, the jewel presented to our family by Louis XIV which traditionally is given to the bride of the second son of the house at their betrothal. And you chose to wear it to spend an evening with a complete stranger. Can you wonder that the evening was not as pleasant as you no doubt anticipated?'

He spoke softly, but there was no mistaking the throb of anger in his voice. And in this case, Lissa recognised, his anger was justified.

'I'm sorry,' she said, her voice shaking. 'I had no idea then what the brooch meant, or even that it was valuable. I wore it that night against my better judgement, although I can't expect you to believe that now, and I was never happy about it. I did give it back the next day, and told Paul he had no right to give it to me without first explaining its significance.'

'If it comes to that, Paul had no right to remove it from the rest of the family jewels without my permission,' the Comte's even voice reminded her.

'Perhaps,' Lissa tried to calm her quivering senses. 'But that is a matter between the two of you. I am not to blame for that.'

'If you had had the decency to remain in London and accept your separation from Paul, there would have been no need to raise the matter again,' he said. 'But to return to that evening, it seemed my only course as matters had proceeded as far as an engagement between you was to convince Paul once and for all of the type of woman you were. I would not allow him to ruin his life as—' his voice faltered a little for the first time—'as I—have seen others ruined.'

Lissa glanced at him puzzled. The anger had momentarily been replaced by a different emotion, a bitterness that she sensed was not for once directed at herself.

Frowning slightly, he resumed, 'Paul is displeased with me at the moment because I have taken him from a life of idleness, and he has to work for his living for the first time. But I have never given him cause to doubt my word, and if I had shown him the brooch, and told him it was proof of your physical infidelity to him with his own brother, that would have ended his feeling for you, I think.'

'You—devil,' Lissa said softly.

'It may be better not to start calling each other names,' he said calmly. 'Allow me to escort you back to the Chateau so that you can pack your things.'

Lissa's lips parted to utter a protest, or at least to attempt some explanation of her present relationship with Paul, but before she could speak, a musical voice exclaimed, 'Ah, *mes enfants*! Then you have met,' and Madame de Gue joined them.

'Raoul,' she shook her head at him, frowning playfully, 'I might have known I would find you at the stables. Why did you not come in to tea to meet our guests?'

'My business with Everard finished rather later than I expected,' he explained. 'Madame Desmond arrived safely, I trust?'

'Of course. *Elle est très charmante, très gentille*,' Madame said smilingly. 'Only think, Raoul, she has been so good as to sign all my copies of her novels. And you, *ma petite*,' she turned her gaze on Lissa. 'Do you also write, or are you content to leave such things to your godmother?'

'I used to write children's stories for my friends when I was small.' Lissa forced herself to speak normally. She remembered Paul saying that his mother's health was not robust, and she was anxious not to upset her by giving any hint of the scene that had just passed between Raoul and herself. 'I've never had the urge to see myself in print, though. I like helping Maggie—my godmother—with her research, and of course this invitation was a wonderful opportunity for her,' she added breathlessly, very conscious of Raoul de Gue's dark eyes watching her intently.

There was a short pause, then Lissa rushed into speech again. 'I hope you don't mind my exploring, *madame*. I didn't intend to find the stables. I got a bit lost, actually, because I was really looking for the little walled garden I can see from my bedroom window.'

'*Oh là*, you English and your gardens!' Madame de Gue laughed. 'It was planted, as you may guess, by Raoul's grandmother. She had—what is the English phrase?—"green fingers". Anne Marie tends the garden when she is at home, and that of course is not as

62

often as I could wish.'

She paused and looked searchingly at Lissa. 'Are you sure the journey has not overtired you, *petite*? She looks pale, does she not, Raoul?'

'A little, perhaps.' His voice gave nothing away.

Oddly, Lissa found this apparent indifference harder to bear than even his anger and contempt. She wanted to escape, to get back to the privacy of her room and give way to the tears that were again threatening to engulf her.

'Poor little one,' Madame de Gue looked at her compassionately. 'Such a long journey, and in this heat. Raoul, *mon cher*, give Mademoiselle Fairfax your arm back to the house.'

'Oh, no,' Lissa blurted out. 'I—I mean, *merci bien*, but I'm all right really. I'll just go and have a lie down for half an hour, then I'll be fine.'

She forced an unconvincing smile to her trembling lips, then turned and ran back the way she had come as if all the devils in hell were after her.

Once back in her bedroom, she gave way to her tears, and when the storm of weeping eventually subsided, she knew that, as in her childhood, much of the emotion that had inspired it had been purged away. She was coldly angry now as she lay face downward across the bed, tracing the design on the cover with her finger. She had a problem on her hands.

If she did as Raoul de Gue wanted, if she packed and returned to London, then Maggie at least would demand a full explanation. She would not let her secretary go without a struggle. Paul, too, would have to know at least part of the truth, she realised unhappily, and after that there would be little chance of keeping it from Madame de Gue, as Paul's reaction was likely to be explosive, she thought.

She rolled over on to her back with a groan and pressed her hand against her smarting eyes. If only she had obeyed her instincts, all this trouble would have been avoided. Paul's attentions had flattered her, so she had refused to face the fact that she did not really care for him sufficiently to marry him.

But why was this suddenly so clear? she asked herself. Only a week ago, she had been unable to sort out her feelings for Paul, and Jenny had thought them an ideal couple. To be fair to herself, she had not kept him dangling through vanity alone, but through her anxiety to do the right thing and not make a mistake which might damage both their lives. Lissa believed in marriage, but in marriage for life, not for a few tenuous years.

No, she could not just leave, but on the other hand, how in the world was she to stay? Raoul de Gue had misjudged her, but if she was honest, she had to admit she had given him some cause. Her anger at this treatment of her was heightened when she recalled how nearly he had succeeded in destroying her relationship with Paul—and her own self-respect. The memory of her aching response to his lovemaking brought hot humiliated colour to her face. It would be impossible now to convince him that she was not the tarty little gold-digger that he thought her. And why did she even want to?

She sat up pushing her hair away from her face. Whatever he thought of her, there was no excuse for his behaviour. The arrogance of the man! she thought, seething. So sure of his own sex appeal that he thought she would surrender without a murmur. And so she nearly had, said an inner voice. But only because he deliberately saw to it that she drank more than usual, Lissa repudiated the traitorous thought.

She got up and began to pace round the room, her

arms wrapped tightly across her.

Whatever happened, she would not be driven away, and sent back to London in disgrace. After all, she reasoned, it was unlikely that Raoul de Gue would want his mother to know about his underhand activities.

'I'll see Paul as soon as I can and break it to him gently that it's all over between us,' she thought, and felt a sense of relief now that she had arrived at a decision at last.

But she decided she would warn Paul not to say anything to his brother. She would just let him stew until Maggie's work here was finished, and then she would tell him herself that his precious family honour and traditions were going to remain unsmirched.

Having carefully removed all traces of her tears, Lissa took immense care over her appearance at dinner that night. She had decided to wear one of her favourite dresses—a full-length square-necked gown in a deep wine red wool jersey. She coaxed her hair into a smooth knot at the nape of her neck and softened the resulting severe line with a pair of deeply fringed silver ear-rings.

When she was ready, she went along to Maggie's room and tapped on the door.

'Come in!' Maggie called cheerfully. 'Well,' she swung round on her dressing stool as Lissa obeyed. 'You've pulled out all the stops tonight, my pet. Going into competition with *la belle Vaumont*?'

'Good lord,' Lissa said, appalled, 'I'd forgotten all about her!'

Maggie chuckled. 'How flattered she would be to hear that! I guarantee you won't have been out of her thoughts much since we left her poisoning the air with those weird cigarettes of hers.' She stood up, slim and attractive in a long skirt and matching over-blouse of blue and gold lamé. 'Well, I'm ready if you are. To the lions, oh, Christian, though why I should say that, heaven knows. Madame is an angel, isn't she, and I can't wait to meet the mysterious Comte—whatever his name may be. Paul hasn't mentioned it, has he?'

'Raoul,' Lissa supplied reluctantly. She saw Maggie's eyebrows lift in surprise and went on hastily, 'I—he—we met in the stables earlier on—quite by accident.'

'Ho-hum!' Maggie eyed her quizzically. 'Something tells me it must have been quite an encounter to bring that glint to your eye. Don't tell me about it now. It might spoil my appetite, and I have a suspicion that the cuisine in this establishment is going to demand that we complement it with calm minds and unimpaired digestions.'

Lissa laughed, and they linked arms companionably as they started on their way downstairs.

Madame de Gue had not yet appeared in the small salon for cocktails, and there was no sign of Paul or the Comte either, Lissa was glad to note. But the room was occupied. A dark-haired little girl in a green dress was sitting in one of the high-backed chairs, feet dangling. As Lissa and Maggie walked in, she slid hastily to the ground and bobbed a curtsy.

'*Bon soir, madame. Bon soir, mademoiselle.*' She had a quiet, grave little voice. Her long hair had been plaited and the plaits wound into a coronet on top of her head. It was too grown-up a style for a child who could not have been more than seven or eight years old, but oddly enough it suited her, Lissa thought, and at the same time, with a slight pang, what a wistful little face.

Maggie, who liked children, and usually attracted them to her, took her hand and spoke to her pleasantly, admiring her dress and asking her name, which was

66

Françoise.

Where does she fit into the set-up? Lissa wondered. Madame had spoken of only one daughter, and she did not really think it feasible for Madame herself to have a child of that age. Besides, she was almost sure that Paul had told her his father had been dead for at least ten years.

At that moment the salon door opened, and Dominique walked in. Her glance flickered round, taking in the occupants of the room, and her movement checked slightly for a moment. Lissa guessed with amusement that she would have liked to have turned on her heel and walked straight out again, but lacked sufficient nerve.

Dominique looked enchanting in an organdie dress with a black bodice and many-tiered white skirt, each frill of which was edged in black. She looked like an ultra-sophisticated Pierrette. Françoise was lost in admiration of it as Lissa and Maggie murmured civil greetings and received in return a *'Bon soir'* that was curt to the point of rudeness. It wasn't long before Françoise sidled close to Dominique, who had taken a cigarette from a silver box on a low table and was rummaging in her small black evening bag for a lighter.

Hesitantly, Françoise put out a hand and touched one of the frills on the skirt.

'Your dress is beautiful, Dominique,' she said shyly.

'But not for long, with your fingermarks all over it,' was the biting reply.

The child's face crimsoned, and she turned immediately and went back to the chair she had occupied when Lissa first saw her.

Lissa was just preparing to give the other girl a piece of her mind, when she encountered a warning frown from Maggie and subsided. After all, they were all

67

guests, and Dominique seemed to be an old friend of the family. 'And that's the last thing I could be described as,' Lissa thought with an inward chuckle.

In the inward silence that followed, Dominique walked with conscious grace to one of the brocaded sofas and sat down, wreathing herself in pungent smoke. Lissa glanced at Françoise, but the child's eyes were fixed on the carpet, and she was biting her lip. It was a relief to hear voices and laughter, signalling the arrival of Madame de Gue and Paul.

'*Je suis en retard.* Forgive me,' Madame smiled round, then held out her hand to Françoise. '*Viens, petite.*'

The child ran to her eagerly and gave her a kiss, receiving a warm hug in return.

Madame de Gué apparently assumed that Dominique had made them aware of the child's identity, for she made no further introductions, but led the little girl to her usual seat by the fire. This, Lissa thought, was an evening ritual, because Françoise pulled out a small footstool from under the chair and sat down on it at Madame's feet, resting her head against her legs.

'Where is Mademoiselle Firaud?' Madame asked.

'She is having dinner in her room. Another headache.' And Françoise gave her head a little toss of disgust.

'I hope you have been behaving yourself,' Madame remarked.

'*Ah, oui.* I have been so good that I am going to ask Papa if he will excuse me from lessons tomorrow and let me go riding with him instead.'

Lissa was conscious of a sense of shock. Paul, busy at the cocktail cabinet mixing martinis, was clearly not Papa. Who else was there? She knew the answer as if it had been spelled out for her. Françoise was Raoul de Gue's child. But in that case, where was his wife? Why wasn't she doing the honours as chatelaine instead of his mother?

Paul brought her a drink, and she thanked him with a swift mechanical smile, not even noticing the look of concern he gave her.

She could not understand why she felt so disturbed at the evidence that Raoul de Gue was married and a father. There had been nothing at all in their brief but stormy acquaintance to suggest that he was anything but single, and her face burned suddenly. He must have left his wife in Paris, she reasoned, but if so, why was the child here and not with her mother?

She took a sip of her drink and noticed with horror that her hand was shaking. She felt a quiver suddenly run along her nerve endings, and it did not need Françoise's hopeful little cry 'Papa!' to tell her that Raoul de Gue, tall and immaculate in evening clothes, had entered the room. The child flung herself at him rapturously, but he did not embrace her, merely patting her cheek and telling her to resume her seat.

Lissa busied herself with a pretence of looking in her bag for a handkerchief while the Comte was being introduced to Maggie. She was dreading the moment when she would be obliged to speak to him again.

'Good evening, Mademoiselle Fairfax. I trust you have now recovered from your journey.'

That was it. No hidden meanings or sarcastic inflections. Just a simple query by a courteous host, and to her everlasting shame Lissa blushed to the roots of her hair, and murmured something inaudible in reply.

Paul, his drinks dispensed, came and sat by her.

'So you have met my dear brother,' he whispered. 'Don't be overwhelmed by the grand manner. He can be human, but being the Comte and a successful businessman as well goes to his head at times. You have made a hit with Maman.'

'She's a lovely person,' Lissa said with absolute sincerity, thankful that Paul did not probe too deeply into her reactions to the Comte. She smiled at her delightedly.

'I knew you would adore her,' he said. 'Lissa, let me tell her—about us. It would make her very happy, I know.'

He had taken her hand, but Lissa withdrew it sharply from his grasp. As she did so, her eyes met those of Raoul de Gue, who was standing by the hearth, one arm resting negligently on the overmantel. His gaze was enigmatic, but she knew he had seen her swift movement, and to her horror, she felt herself colouring again.

'Paul,' she murmured agitatedly, 'not now. Please! I—I can't tell you about it here, but we'll talk tomorrow.'

'As you wish, *chérie*.' Paul's tone was bewildered. 'What is it, Lissa? Something has happened to disturb you. Tell me . . .'

'No, there's nothing.' She gave him a bright determined smile. 'I think I need some fresh air. Do you think anyone would mind if I went out on the terrace for a little while?'

'Of course not. Shall I come with you?'

'No, Paul. I'd rather be on my own for a while.'

The inevitable *tête-à-tête* had better be postponed until they were completely out of range of the Comte's speculative gaze, she thought.

Paul escorted her to the heavy satin curtains that had been drawn across the long windows that led to the terrace and opened them for her. In spite of her request for solitude, she guessed he intended to make another attempt to accompany her, and felt guiltily pleased when Dominique halted him with an imperious request for another drink.

Even Dominique has her uses, Lissa reflected callously, as she crossed the terrace and stood by the wide parapet looking towards the valley. It was quite dusk by this time—a windless evening, and pleasantly warm.

Lissa began to feel peacefully relaxed. She leaned against the cool stone and watched the silver splash of the fountain in the courtyard below.

It was that sudden tingling of the nerves again that told her she was not alone any longer.

'You left your drink.' His voice was non-committal. That confrontation in the stableyard might have happened to two other people on a different planet, she thought confusedly as she accepted the glass with a word of formal thanks. He did not return to the salon at once, as she had half expected, but came to lean on the parapet beside her.

'Why do you stare at a view that it is too dark to see?' he inquired after a few moments of unnerving silence.

'I saw the view today. I wanted to see how the night changes things.' She was embarrassed at finding herself alone with him and furious with herself for being embarrassed.

'Ah,' he said quietly. There was another pause. 'A lot of things can change in the course of a day—and a night—can they not?'

Now they were back to the hidden meanings again, Lissa thought angrily. She faced him.

'Forgive me, Monsieur le Comte, but I'm a little tired of these cat-and-mouse games of yours. I feel I should tell you that in spite of what was said this afternoon I've no intention of leaving my employer and returning to London. I'm sure you realise that to do so will be to involve us both in some very long and embarrassing explanations. I expect to be very busy from tomorrow and no doubt you will be returning to

Paris and your business there. I'll do my best to keep out of your way while you are here, and be as un-obtrusive as possible, but . . .'

She was interrupted by the certainty that he was laughing, although he made no sound and his face was shadowed by one of the tall stone urns standing on the parapet. She stood, her hands clenched, for once com-pletely at a loss. How could she deal with a man who seemed to change his attitude to her as easily as she changed her clothes?

'Forgive me,' he said after a moment, and by the tremor in his voice, she knew her suspicions were cor-rect. 'But the thought of you being unobtrusive, Mademoiselle Fairfax I find entirely captivating. The fact is, *ma belle*, that you are far too lovely to be any-thing but obtrusive, and I suspect you know it. It is far too late for you to try and merge into the background now.'

'Under the circumstances, flattery from you, *mon-sieur*, is merely adding insult to injury,' Lissa flashed back at him.

There was another silence. Lissa stood, biting her lip, uncertain whether to go or stand her ground. Although he did not seem to be launching another attack at her immediately, she found even his silent presence disturbing and unnerving. His behaviour too seemed contradictory, and it was infuriating to realise that she had never known exactly where she was with him from their first meeting. She had always been at a disadvantage, and she was determined to be so no longer. To run away now would be another defeat.

She swallowed some of her drink and stared un-seeingly into the gathering darkness, desperately con-scious of the tall figure lounging beside her. She was so keyed up that when he did speak again, she started and spilled a little of the liquid from her glass.

'How long have you worked for Madame Desmond?' he asked unexpectedly.

Lissa's impulse was to tell him childishly to mind his own business, but she controlled herself.

'I have been her secretary since I came to live in London two years ago,' she said, deliberately making her tone as cool as possible in order to dissuade him from further questions. But he appeared oblivious to the hint.

'And is she aware how your spare time is spent?'

'She knows that I read, visit friends, go to the theatre and cinema and wash my hair,' Lissa said bitingly. 'Is that what you mean?'

'You know quite well that is not what I mean.' His voice bit back at her. 'Does she know about your—social life? That you will go out with men of whom you know nothing?'

'How dare you!' Lissa flared. 'Of course Maggie knows I have dates with men, and she knows I've been on blind dates in my time. There are probably few of my generation that haven't.'

'I would assume the reason is not too far to seek,' he said. 'I assume it is a question of money. Your salary may be adequate, but it hardly pays for the kind of high life you seem to enjoy. I suppose the chance of a free dinner every now and then ...'

'To hell with you and your assumptions!' Lissa's anger made her completely reckless of the consequences. 'What right have you to become a judge of my actions, and how dare you suppose that I'm short of money and need that sort of dirty—charity? Maggie pays me very well, let me tell you, and if ever I got into a mess financially I have my parents to turn to. I certainly have no need to let strange men buy me dinner, so that thay can buy me in return. Jenny and I live quite comfortably, and no one has ever dared to suggest the kind of—vileness about me that you seem to believe. Jenny was horrified when I told her what had happened that night.'

'You told her about me?' He sounded incredulous.

'Of course I did,' she flung back at him. 'What did you expect?'

'You could not imagine,' he said slowly, 'that I was merely some Continental wolf...'

'You are not the only one to make assumptions, Monsieur le Comte.' For the first time in their relationship, Lissa felt as if she stood on equal terms with him. She did not know what reaction to expect, but it was certainly not the amused chuckle and murmur of 'Touché' that came from the darkness surrounding him.

She stood feeling oddly baffled and more than a little angry. What an unpredictable creature he was! She glanced towards the lighted windows of the salon and shivered a little ostentatiously.

'It's getting rather cold. I think I'll go in,' she began, and was startled to feel his hand reaching to grip her arm.

'Un moment,' he said softly, but with a note of command. 'There are only a few moments left before dinner and I have something important I wish to ask.'

Lissa's former nervousness began to return. She tried to free her arm, but he would not relax his grip and his touch was having a disconcerting effect on her. She forced her voice to remain controlled.

'At your service, Monsieur le Comte.'

He was standing so close to her now that if she had so much as swayed their bodies would have touched. She stood rigid, acutely conscious of him, of his warmth and the faint expensive smell of the cologne he used.

'Flattering, but scarcely true,' His voice was sarcastic. 'However, it is the truth I require, as you seem to be in a mood for frankness. Are you in fact engaged to my brother?'

Lissa wanted to fling back a defiant 'Yes,' but her quivering lips would not frame the word.

'I am awaiting your reply, *mademoiselle*.' There was an urgent note in his voice. 'I must—know.'

She stood staring up at him, trying vainly to read his expression. Her heart was hammering, and she felt suddenly weary of sparring with him.

'I'm not engaged to Paul,' she said. 'I—I never have been.'

They stood, the silence between them almost tangible. Lissa felt in some kind of dream. She wanted to step back away from the tall figure that seemed poised over her like a hawk ready to swoop, but she was imprisoned between his body and the balustrade.

Slowly his fingers relaxed their grip and slid up her arm to her shoulder before coming to rest lightly against the pulse in her throat.

'Are you in love with him?' He was almost whispering.

Lissa moistened her parted lips to reply, but at that moment Françoise's voice called, 'Papa—mademoiselle! Dinner is served!'

'Coming, *petite*.' His voice at its normal level woke Lissa from the trance-like state that had held her. 'I must go in,' she thought wildly.

'Wait,' he said, his hand gripping her shoulder again. 'You have not yet answered my question.'

'I have no intention of doing so.' Lissa tore herself free. 'You have my assurance that there is no engagement. My emotions are my own concern. And now, please excuse me. I—I want my dinner.'

'But of course.' His tone was mocking as he waved her towards the salon. '*Bon appetit, ma belle*.'

# CHAPTER FIVE

DINNER was not a comfortable meal for Lissa, and she knew afterwards she had done less than justice to an excellent meal. As they made their way to the dining room she saw that Paul was trying to get to her side, obviously bursting with curiosity about the conversation with the Comte. She was relieved to find that she was not sitting next to him at the table. 'I couldn't bear another inquisition,' she thought.

In fact, she had been placed next to Françoise, who was subdued if polite company. Lissa was amazed to see the child managing the various courses and their complementary wines as if she was a sophisticated adult. She was not sure she totally approved of this facet of French upbringing, but she remembered being told that French children were taught to behave impeccably in public, and certainly Françoise was a credit to her training.

Dominique tended to monopolise the conversation, and as she used her own language a good deal, Lissa found it rather hard to follow. The de Gues must have been aware of this, because they all spoke English, but if Dominique realised she was being given a hint, she chose to ignore it. She was sitting next to Paul, and if Lissa had not been feeling so strung up and disturbed she could have derived some private amusement counting the number of times that Dominique found it necessary to touch him, either by putting her hand on his arm or leaning coquettishly towards him. Paul himself was silent and unresponsive to these manoeuvres.

'I have asked for coffee to be served in the gallery,'

Raoul de Gue was saying. 'I hope you are not too tired, *madame*, to look at our treasures tonight.'

'No indeed.' Maggie dropped her table napkin briskly on to the table. 'I'm looking forward to it.'

Lissa's heart sank. She had intended to plead a headache and slip away early to her room, but she knew Maggie would expect her to accompany them to the gallery, if only to look at the portraits.

The walls of the gallery were white, and each portrait was individually lit. Lissa looked with particular interest at Comte Henry who had fled the Revolution, that killed his father, to find safety in England and bring back an English bride. There was an indisputable family likeness, Lissa thought, noting the thin high-bridged nose and uncompromising chin of the man in the portrait. Exchange his high-waisted coat and cravat for a dinner jacket and black tie and it could be Raoul de Gue who stood surveying his descendants with a well-bred sneer. Arrogant brute, she decided, turning with a feeling of sympathy to the gentle fair-haired girl in the next portrait in the Empire style gown who had helped rebuild the family fortunes, as well as the Chateau.

'It was a love match. They were utterly devoted to each other,' Raoul's voice said behind her. He sounded faintly amused, as if he could guess what she was thinking. 'I bet!' she thought, seething.

There were glass showcases and cabinets set round the walls between the pictures, containing miniatures and pieces of valuable china and porcelain. The coffee had been set out on a large circular table in the middle of the gallery, which also held, to Lissa's dismay, a number of flat velvet-covered cases.

Paul who had disappeared a few moments before came back carrying two large silver candelabra. He put them on the table and lit the candles, then, as they gathered round the table, the gallery lights went out.

'Forgive the melodrama,' Raoul said, smiling. 'Candlelight seems more effective for these pieces.' He picked up the largest of the velvet cases and opened it. The flames of the candles were picked up and reflected back in a new spectrum of light and fire in the diamonds and emeralds of the most exquisite necklace Lissa had ever seen. She could not even guess at its value.

'This is the de Gue necklace.' Madame la Comtesse took it lovingly from its satin bed and held it for a moment against the low neckline of her grey silk evening dress so that they could see the effect. 'Yes, I have worn it—on my wedding day and on other special occasions, but *hélas*, it is too valuable to be seen as often as it deserves.'

Lissa had a sudden disturbing vision of another bride, veiled and mysterious, with the necklace gleaming on her white gown, walking to where Raoul de Gue waited smiling at a shadowy altar. She looked down and found she was gripping the table so tightly that her knuckles were white.

She released the table and stepped back out of the betraying candlelight, but her movement had been noticed. Across the table, Raoul's eyes caught hers and held them for an endless moment. It was as if they were alone. Useless now to deny what her clamouring senses were telling her. Impossible to forget, or to tell herself that he had forgotten that shortlived but magical fusing of their bodies that night in London, no matter what the motive behind it might have been. Lissa only knew that if he stretched out his arms to her now, she would be compelled to go to him.

'And this brooch,' said Madame de Gue, 'is always given to the bride of the second son. It is a charming piece—though not of the same value as the necklace, *naturellement.'*

Lissa looked stupidly at the jewel now being displayed. Of course, Paul would have put it back, she thought. Somehow she had never expected to see it again. And worst of all, Paul was leaning forward smiling significantly and trying to catch her eye.

'These bracelets,' said Raoul, his voice totally expressionless, 'were given to the Comtesse of his day by François I—regrettably, it is believed, for services rendered.'

Lissa had not expected to sleep, but physical weariness overcame her confused and restless emotional state. She awoke to find the room rosy with sunlight, and a smiling Mathilde bringing her a breakfast tray of coffee and croissants. Not a bad way to start the day, by any means, Lissa thought appreciatively, helping herself to cherry jam.

Her meal finished, she showered and dressed and went in search of Maggie, whom she found sitting by the window in her bedroom engrossed in a shabby leather-bound book.

Maggie looked up smiling. 'The famous diary,' she said.

'As interesting as you hoped?'

'Even more so, I think, although reading and translating is a slow business,' Maggie said with a sigh. 'I'd certainly like to think someone could still read my handwriting in almost two hundred years' time.'

'Or even the following day,' Lissa said wickedly, and dodged a playful punch aimed at her ribs. 'Did you do any work last night?'

'Very little. What there is, I've put in that yellow file on the dressing table.'

It had been established at dinner the previous night, rather to Lissa's dismay, that Maggie and she would use the Comte's own library for their work, and the typewriter and other equipment had already been placed there in readiness.

Lissa was relieved that the room's rightful owner was nowhere to be seen. She looked round curiously for any clues to his personality. Her first thought was that it was an essentially masculine room, and a working man's room at that, with an immense desk, which came in for a great deal of use, judging by the papers that littered it. There was a filing cabinet, and a large glass-fronted cupboard on one wall, and the other three were lined with books. There were no pictures, and Lissa noticed particularly no photographs.

Again she found herself speculating as to what kind of a woman Françoise's mother was—and where she was. Certainly she had made no impression on this rather stark room.

Lost in her thoughts, she started at a light tap on the door.

'*Entrez!*' she called, and Madame Barrat appeared, beaming.

'I came to see that you have everything you need, *mademoiselle.*'

'I think so, thank you,' Lissa said gratefully. 'It's very good of the Comte to give up his room like this.'

'It is rarely used now by anyone but Monsieur, and he is nearly always in Paris,' Madame commented. 'Monsieur Paul has his own bureau on the estate, and Mademoiselle Anne-Marie likes to leave her work behind her in Paris.'

'And the Comte's wife?'

'*Comment?*' Madame Barrat stared at Lissa. '*Ah, non, mademoiselle.* Madame was so rarely here. She preferred to live in Paris also, *la pauvre.* I doubt if she ever set foot in this room.'

'You speak in the past.'

'*Vraiment, mademoiselle.*' Madame Barrat sighed. 'Madame was killed six years ago when *la petite* Françoise was only *deux ans.*'

'How awful! I had no idea.' Lissa spread out her hands helplessly. 'You said she was killed. Was there some accident?'

'A terrible accident, *mademoiselle. La petite* was sick and Madame set out to come to her. Her car was struck by a lorry and Madame was killed outright. *Quelle horreur!*' She shuddered. 'Monsieur le Comte was like a man distraught. For weeks he would see no one, or allow what had happened to be mentioned in his hearing.'

'What was she like?' Lissa asked quietly.

'*Très belle. Très chic,*' said Madame Barrat. 'She was dark, of course, and her clothes were always—*formidable.* She worked for a couture house before they were married—that was how they met. It was little wonder that she found St Denis so dull after the world of *haute couture.*'

Dull, Lissa thought wonderingly. She had a vivid picture of Raoul's dark attractiveness, and Françoise's wistful little face, and to her horror, felt tears pricking her eyelids. She turned hurriedly away from Madame's shrewd gaze and began to sort the papers on the desk into neat piles.

'Will Monsieur mind if I put these on top of the filing cabinet for safety?' she asked.

'He said you were to make what arrangements seemed best to you, *mademoiselle.*' Madame Barrat turned to go and then checked for a moment. 'And Madame la Comtesse hopes you will join her and Madame Desmond for *café* at eleven on clock.'

Lissa found that Maggie had spoken less than the truth when she had said she had done very little work the previous night. There was quite enough to keep her well occupied right up to eleven, and when the gilded clock above the fireplace struck the hour, she was glad of the break.

But as she was crossing the hall, she heard Paul calling her name urgently. He came up to her and took her arm.

'Come into the garden for a moment,' he said rapidly. 'I must talk to you.'

'But I'm supposed to be having coffee with your mother,' Lissa began.

'This is important,' he said impatiently. 'I must see you in private.'

It was pleasant in the garden, but Lissa, stealing a glance at Paul's sullen angry face, deduced that there were storms in the offing.

'Did Raoul talk to you about me last night?' he demanded.

'He did mention you,' Lissa admitted cautiously. Her memories of the previous day were completely overshadowed by that moment of revelation in the gallery and its disastrous aftermath.

'Did he ask if we were going to be married?'

'Yes,' Lissa said, puzzled. 'But I told him we weren't.'

Paul swore explosively under his breath.

'Paul,' Lissa swung on him. 'I warned you in London that I was coming here only on the understanding that there were no strings between us. And—and I'm glad to be talking to you like this, because there is something I must tell you.'

'And there is something I must tell you,' Paul said savagely. 'Monsieur le Comte, my brother, has informed me that he wishes me to marry Dominique.'

Lissa caught her breath and stared at him.

'You think I'm joking?' he asked. 'It's only too true, I assure you.' He laughed bitterly. 'Her father is a wealthy manufacturer of textiles, you understand.

Raoul has plans for mass market production of some of the Fontaine designs. It would be far more convenient for these plans if the Vaumont complex was part of the family.'

'But that's utterly feudal!' Lissa burst out. 'He can't expect...'

'Can't expect?' Paul echoed. 'Oh, you don't know my brother, *chérie*. I guessed he was up to something when he followed you last night. I was summoned to the presence this morning and told precisely what he expected me to do. I protested, of course, and told him I was going to marry you. He said he had your word that you would not be my wife.'

'That isn't strictly correct,' Lissa said quickly. 'I told him we were not engaged, that's all.'

'Lissa,' Paul seized her hands, his face alight, 'you're the only person who can help me. If I tell him that we are engaged after all...'

'No!' Lissa looked at him, horrified. 'That's out of the question. All you have to do is stand up to him.'

'Oh, it's easy to say that,' Paul said hopelessly. 'You forget, *ma chère*, I'm dependent on him for everything —my food, my clothes even, and my job.'

'Paul,' said Lissa gently, 'I'm sorry to have to choose this moment, but I did say I had something to tell you. You have to know that I've made up my mind about us. Marriage wouldn't work for us, and I'm even surer now after the things you have been saying. I'm very fond of you, but that's not enough—well, not enough for me, anyway.'

'I think I always knew you would say that,' Paul said. He touched her cheek briefly and regretfully with his lips, then swung away. '*Mon Dieu*! What am I going to do?'

Lissa watched him, frowning a little. She was frankly taken aback by his calm acceptance of her decision not to marry him. She had not wanted him to be heartbroken, but she had at least expected some reaction, she told herself.

A number of odd circumstances were now recalled to her mind. Dominique's possessiveness, for instance, and her mention of letters that had passed between them. An unwelcome suspicion was beginning to form in her mind. Had Paul begun his headlong courtship of herself to provide himself with an escape route from a relationship with Dominique which had perhaps grown less desirable as time went on?

She remembered her own doubts about the speed with which he had tried to urge her into an engagement. She still believed he was genuinely fond of her, but she wondered if the flames of this fondness might not have been fanned by his urgent need to extricate himself from Dominique's clutches.

'I don't know what you're going to do,' she said at last. 'And I'm beginning to think that I don't care very much. No one can force you to marry anyone in this day and age, and you know it. You're a grown man, and you could be independent if you wanted. You must have given your brother at some time the idea that you wouldn't object to marrying Dominique. I can't believe he just dreamed the whole thing up—like another fashion design.'

The guilty expression that fleetingly crossed Paul's face convinced her that she had hit a tender spot.

'I admit I found her attractive once, when she came back from Switzerland,' he said. 'But I soon found out what she was really like. Lissa, even if you hated me, and you say you don't—you couldn't wish to see me married to that little . . .'

'I'm not sure you don't deserve each other,' Lissa said coldly. 'Anyway, I have more typing to do. Let me know how you sort things out. I shall be fascinated.'

'Lissa,' he halted her again, 'would you consider at least pretending to be my fiancée? I would hold you to nothing once the danger was past.'

'And when would that be?' Lissa was really angry now. 'When Dominique marries someone else, I suppose? And what precisely am I to do in the meantime? Just hang about living a lie for your benefit? You have one hell of a nerve!'

'Yes,' he admitted frankly. 'But I am desperate.'

'I'm not,' Lissa said cruelly, and walked away.

She was still seething with temper when she reached the house. She went straight to the Comte's library. The door was partly open and Raoul de Gue was inside talking on the telephone. Lissa turned away, intending to return later when her attention was caught by what he was saying.

'That little affair of Paul's has been settled, and I can't see it will cost us a sou,' he said. 'At one time I really thought he was going to throw himself away on the little fool, but I think I have been quite clever.'

Lissa found she was holding the door handle so tightly that she had hurt her fingers. She felt sick and humiliated. How easily she had let herself be manipulated the night before! The contempt in his voice this morning was in marked contrast to what, absurdly, she had thought she heard last night.

'I'll see you later, then, *chérie*. It may all work out as we hoped after all. I must go now. *Au revoir*.'

She heard the receiver replaced, and turning fled blindly up the stairs to her own room.

'I'll make the announcement at dinner tonight,' Paul said jubilantly. 'Lissa, you're an angel! But what made you change your mind?'

'It doesn't matter,' said Lissa, her voice sounding like a stranger's. 'Just as long as you remember that I have no intention of marrying you now or ever. But I'll pretend to be your fiancée for the next few weeks until we go back to England, although I hate the idea of deceiving your mother like this.'

'Oh, Maman will understand. I'll tell her all about it afterwards,' Paul said confidently. 'She doesn't care too much for Dominique either.' He laughed exultantly. 'If Raoul still wants the families to merge as well as the businesses, he will have to do the honours himself.'

'Yes,' said Lissa. How hard it was to make the muscles of her throat work properly.

'I can't wait to see Raoul's face when this bombshell goes off tonight,' Paul was saying gleefully. 'It will be perfect. My sister is coming from Paris for the weekend, so there will be a real family party.'

Lissa had never felt less like any sort of party, family or otherwise. Now that her anger and hurt were beginning to subside, she was wondering if she had been too hasty. Upsetting Raoul's plans had seemed the obvious revenge, but it had brought her no satisfaction. Paul was the only one who was pleased. And it had done nothing to salve the aching hurt that had been with her all day. Fortunately she'd had little time to think. Maggie had descended on her like a whirlwind at the end of the morning, and she had a mountain of dictation to transcribe.

'I think the air here suits me,' Maggie had announced joyously. 'I'm going to enjoy doing this book.'

Lissa's only feeling was that the French Revolution had not been sweeping enough, in allowing even one de Gue to escape the guillotine.

'Who was it said that revenge is sweet?' she wondered as she looked into her dressing-table mirror while she was getting ready for dinner. The pale strained face that looked back seemed to have nothing to do with her at all with the girl who had woken so lightheartedly that morning. 'Will the real Lissa Fairfax please stand up?' she thought wryly.

She chose a black dress, high-necked and full-skirted with floating diaphanous sleeves. 'I look as if I'm in mourning,' she thought, but it was too late to change, and Maggie was already tapping at the door and asking if she was ready.

'Not quite,' Lissa called. 'I'll only be a few minutes!'

It was untrue. She simply did not want to have to go down and face them all, including this new sister she had never met, and hear Paul drop his bombshell. But she could not skulk in her room for ever. She had brought it all on herself by her desire for revenge on Raoul.

As she was going out of the door, she stumbled across something on the floor just outside. It seemed to be a large parcel. She picked it up and took it back into her room. The paper it was wrapped in was expensive-looking, with grey and silver stripes, and when she looked closely Lissa saw an elaborate 'F' motif like a watermark in the silver. A white envelope had been pushed into a fold of the parcel with her name on it. It contained a card.

'To make amends for the one I tore. R.'

Lissa tore off the paper and the fabric spilled out of her hands and down to the rose-coloured carpet. It was blue—the deep blue of a night sky in summer, misted with silver like a scattering of stars. She could hear Max Prentiss's genial voice. 'Midsummer Night—against that hair, eh, Raoul?'

Hastily, her hands shaking, she bundled the fabric and the card back into the wrapping paper and pushed the whole parcel into one of the fitted wardrobes. It could be found there, after she had gone, she told herself.

The salon seemed full when Lissa entered. Anne-Marie de Gue was a slim twenty-two-year-old, as dark as her elder brother, with a pretty, mobile face. She had Françoise on her knee and their heads were bent absorbedly over a picture book.

Paul performed the necessary introductions, then led Lissa to the corner of the room on the pretext of mixing her a drink.

'You look very pale, *chérie*,' he whispered.

'I feel very pale.' Lissa looked at him in appeal. 'Paul, I don't think this is such a good idea after all. Deceiving your mother, even for a little while, and everyone else. And now your sister is here as well. Surely there must be some other way of making it plain to Raoul—and Dominique if need be—that the marriage is off.'

'Lissa, you can't let me down! You gave me your word...'

'Yes, but I shouldn't have done. I was—upset.'

It was on the tip of her tongue to let Paul know about the snatch of conversation she had overheard, but she decided against it. Relations between Paul and Raoul were already strained, it seemed, and life would be difficult enough before the evening was over without telling tales.

'But you did promise,' he persisted. 'And I won't hold you to it when this affair has blown over. I swear it. Please, Lissa. Maman—her heart is not strong, and when Raoul and I quarrel, she is upset. This way, there will be no quarrel. Raoul can say nothing.'

Oh, can't he? Lissa thought, twisting her hands miserably together. 'All right,' she said at last. 'I'll go through with it—but for no longer than absolutely necessary. And I am not going to behave as if I were in fact your fiancée.' And she gave Paul a long level look:

'*Mon ange*!' he breathed, and before she could prevent him, he kissed her cheek lightly. Her face flaming, Lissa looked round to see if anyone had noticed. She immediately encountered a look of glittering dislike from Dominique who had just entered with, Lissa saw with a sinking heart, Raoul de Gue. His own glance was enigmatic, but she knew he had seen Paul's caress. She lifted her chin and returned his gaze with a defiance she was far from feeling.

She was continually on edge during the meal that followed, waiting for Paul to make the announcement. When she saw champagne brought in, she laid down her knife and fork, feeling she would choke if she took another mouthful.

'There is a celebration.' Madame de Gue leaned forward to Raoul smiling, her eyebrows raised.

'Not that I am aware of,' he returned, but Paul interrupted him, rising to his feet.

'*Mais oui*, there is cause to celebrate, Maman,' he said rather too loudly. 'I wish you all to drink the health of Lissa—Mademoiselle Fairfax, who has done me the honour to consent to be my wife.'

There was a stunned silence. Anne-Marie was the first to lift her glass.

'*Mes félicitations*,' she said a little uncertainly.

'Paul, *mon fils*!' Madame de Gue was smiling, but her eyes were puzzled. 'What a surprise to spring on us like this.' She turned towards Lissa. '*Ma chère*, we had no idea.'

'We met in London, ages ago,' Paul said. 'We knew almost at once.'

'We just couldn't decide the best moment to tell you all,' Lissa said a little lamely, trying to smile and play the happy fiancée.

At last she forced herself to look at Raoul de Gue. She had expected anger, contempt, even chagrin. But his face was shadowed, as he leaned back in his chair away from the candlelit table, and she could not read his expression.

Beside him Dominique was making no effort to disguise her fury and resentment at the turn of events and was speaking to him in a low-voiced flood of furious French. As he listened, his fingers idly tracing the slender stem of his glass suddenly tightened. Lissa swallowed. She could almost feel the pressure of those fingers around her throat.

She got up hastily, scraping her chair.

'Please excuse me.' Again she tried to smile. 'I—I have a slight headache—the excitement, I expect. Perhaps you would permit me ...'

Madame de Gue was instantly sympathetic, and promised a hot drink would be sent up. As Lissa passed her chair, she pressed her hand warmly.

'And tomorrow we will have a little *tête-à-tête*,' she whispered with a conspiratorial smile.

Lissa thanked her, feeling wretched, and was glad to escape to her room, leaving Paul to enjoy the sensation he had caused.

But in spite of the hot drink, sleep would not come, and Lissa found that her head was soon aching in earnest. She got out of bed and wandered restlessly to the window, leaning her head against the cool panes. It occurred to her that she still had not found the walled garden which lay keeping its secrets just below. Tomorrow, it might make a splendid refuge from Raoul's anger, Dominique's malevolence and even the Comtesse's desire for a confidential chat. Lissa shuddered.

'What have I got myself into?' she thought frantically. 'I must have been quite mad!'

Then suddenly she tensed. Somewhere near at hand a board had creaked. As she listened, a soft knock came at her door—Maggie, no doubt, who had been as surprised as anyone, come for an explanation of this apparent change of heart. Well, she was entitled to it, particularly as Lissa was supposed to be at the Chateau for the sole purpose of working on this book with her godmother, but she wished she had waited until the morning.

Listlessly she walked across the room to the door. She was reaching for the handle when Raoul de Gue's voice, pitched low, said, 'Mademoiselle!'

Lissa froze instantly. Her mouth felt dry, and she leaned weakly against the panels of the door for support.

'Oh, no,' she thought wildly. 'I can't face him now!'

The knock came again. 'Mademoiselle!' He spoke more loudly. 'I know you are there. Please open the door. I must speak to you at once.'

Lissa's tired brain reeled. What did he mean by coming to her room like this? It was still relatively early and the others were doubtless still in the salon.

She was deeply conscious of her almost transparent nightgown, and the pink-shaded lamp shadowing the rumpled bed with a peculiar intimacy. Her body began to tremble as memories of that night in London came flooding back.

Surely he didn't intend to try those tactics on her again? He couldn't be so despicable. Although she had come to her senses just in time, he must have known the effect he had had on her, she thought dazedly. He must have known it too when he looked at her across the candles in the gallery, and when he had forced her to stand in close proximity to him on the terrace.

She pressed her hand achingly to her mouth. It would be easy to open the door, but she had no doubt what would inevitably follow. He had told her, after all, that he would stop at nothing to break up her relationship with Paul, and he had made it clear what kind of woman he considered her.

'Lissa!' For the first time he breathed her name, with a kind of sensual insistence. 'Open the door now! I must see you.'

She felt the handle move under her fingers as he tried the door. In a flash she threw off the almost trance-like state he seemed able to induce in her, in which surrender to him was not only necessary but desirable. Her hand closed round the ornate key she had barely noticed before, and even as she turned it, the desperate thought came that it might be purely for ornament. But there was a sharp click, and she was safe at least from him, if not from herself.

She stood breathlessly, her cheek pressed against the smooth wood, waiting for him to speak again, but instead she heard quiet footsteps going away.

She stood waiting, endlessly it seemed, but there was no further sound, and slowly she unlocked the door again, allowing the first tears of over-tense nerves and confused emotions to run unchecked down her face.

# CHAPTER SIX

Lissa slept late in the morning. She was awoken by Mathilde bringing her breakfast tray with an air of subdued excitement. Watching the girl fuss with the curtains and hang away last night's discarded dress, Lissa realised she had become a person of importance in the household. It did nothing to help her feeling of guilt.

There was a note on the tray from Maggie. 'Well, ducky, I hope you know what you're doing,' it ran. 'I'm going out with Madame on a tour of the local beauty spots. I want you to relax and get some colour back into those cheeks. I'll see you later.'

Lissa laid down the note and poured herself some coffee. At least she would not have the embarrassment of having to behave to the Comtesse as a future daughter-in-law might be expected to do, yet she did not relish having to spend the day without Maggie's reassuring presence as a barrier against the rest of the world. She had hoped to be able to immerse herself in work to the exclusion of everything else, whereas now it looked as if she would be left to her own devices for most of the day. She sighed deeply, but at that moment her reverie was disturbed by a light tap at the door.

Lissa tensed involuntarily, then relaxed in surprise as Anne-Marie de Gue came in. She was carrying a slender silver vase containing three perfect pink rosebuds, with drops of early morning moisture still clinging to them and she was smiling.

'Are you better? I do hope so, and so does Paul. He was moping quite badly after you left us last night.' Her dark eyes examined Lissa attentively. 'I picked these from Grand'mère's garden. They are early, I know, but it's so sheltered there. The roses come soon and last for ever, she used to say.'

'It's very kind of you,' Lissa said awkwardly. In other circumstances she would have responded eagerly to this overture from at least one member of the family who was not trying to use her in some way.

Anne-Marie shrugged charmingly. 'Well, you are English like her so I thought that roses would appeal to you. They need attention, though. I haven't Grand'mère's touch at pruning time and the whole garden is becoming overgrown because I am so rarely here.'

'Perhaps I could help,' Lissa offered a little shyly. 'I—I like gardening, and used to help at home, although I'm no expert.'

Once again she was subjected to a searching look and then Anne-Marie nodded vigorously.

'A good idea,' she approved. 'A day in the sun will do us both good, and we can get to know each other.' Her manner developed a slight constraint. 'Paul's announcement last night was rather a shock. We—I— had been expecting him to marry someone else—I must be frank.'

'Yes, I know.' Lissa pushed her hair back from her face.

'You knew?' Anne-Marie gazed at her, her brows raised. 'Paul has said, then ... *eh bien*.' She smiled again. 'It will take a little getting used to, you understand.'

'I'm beginning to.' Lissa said slowly. 'I hope it's not too much of a disappointment to everyone.'

'Of course not.' Anne-Marie's tone was warm. 'It is simply that she has loved him ever since they were children together. We always hoped that one day Paul would realise and ... but there, it is wrong to plan everyone's life for them. Paul has chosen you, and soon you will not be a stranger to us any more. When do you plan to be married?'

'It's not decided yet,' said Lissa. She pushed the breakfast tray away and slid out of bed. 'I think I'll get dressed. Perhaps we can do some work in the garden before the sun gets too high.'

'*Certainement*,' Anne-Marie agreed, but with a curious expression in her eyes. 'I will find out where the tools have been kept and wait for you downstairs.' She gave Lissa another encouraging smile and disappeared.

Left to herself, Lissa dressed swiftly in a pair of closely fitting blue levis with a matching denim shirt. She felt like a conspirator as she made her way down to the hall, but to her relief only Anne-Marie was waiting there.

It was a glorious morning and Lissa's spirits rose as she felt the sun on her face. Anne-Marie led the way quickly around the side of the Chateau and along a neat gravelled walk to a gate in a high wall. They passed through and Lissa found herself once more in the stable area. So she had been on the right track after all.

Anne-Marie darted into an outbuilding and emerged a few minutes later with a flat wicker basket holding some elderly-looking trowels and forks and a small pair of shears. She handed this to Lissa and disappeared again. There was a sound of clattering and then she reappeared triumphantly flourishing a hoe, a rake and a small spade.

'Pierre always hides them,' she said gaily. 'He does not approve of women gardening, or of flower gardens, for that matter.'

She led the way out of the courtyard and they turned into a narrow avenue where the trees had been allowed to meet overhead. It was like walking through a cool green tunnel, Lissa thought, and at the end of it was a high grey wall, lichen-covered, with a low arched doorway.

The heavy iron latch, shaped like a lion's head, squeaked protestingly as Anne-Marie lifted it.

Lissa caught her breath. The mass of early summer blooms she had glimpsed from her window above were now set out in front of her like a cluster of jewels in an antique setting. Jostling for attention against the lich-ened walls, Lissa saw old-fashioned English cottage flowers like lupins and delphiniums, but it was the roses that took the eye, and filled the air with their scent, grouped in formal beds round a small over-grown lawn. Beyond the grass a shallow flight of steps led to a small arbour almost hidden in a mass of fragrant jasmine.

'It's like something out of a dream,' Lissa said sniffing the scented air rapturously.

'*Mais oui*,' Anne-Marie agreed. '*En effet*, Grand'-mère used to call this her "*jardin des rêves*"—the garden of dreams. If ever she had a problem, and there were many, you understand, when Fontaine first be-gan, she used to come here and sit, and soon the prob-lem would fade and the answer to it become clear. So she always told us.'

Lissa stood for a moment or two and allowed the peace of the place to have its way with her. Then for the first time since she had come to the Chateau, she threw back her head and laughed out loud, before turning to the mystified Anne-Marie.

'Well, the weeds are one problem that won't be tackled simply by dreaming about them,' she said, smiling. 'We'd better make a start.'

Two back-breaking but companionable hours later they made their way back to the Chateau for lunch, hilariously comparing their blisters but well satisfied with the start they had made. As they separated to wash and change before the meal, Anne-Marie reached out and took Lissa's hands in her own.

'Last night when Paul burst that on us, I did not think I could even like you,' she said, frankly. 'I was wrong. I leap to conclusions—it is a family failing. We are friends now, *non?*'

'Yes, I hope so indeed,' Lissa said sincerely.

The temptation to tell Anne-Marie the truth about her engagement had been almost overwhelming as the morning wore on and, the other girl had chatted about life at the Chateau and general wedding plans, but she felt it would not be fair to Paul to say anything to his sister without consulting him first.

She was puzzled too by Anne-Marie's evident concern for Dominique's feelings. Had Dominique really been in love with Paul since childhood? On the face of what Lissa had seen, it seemed most unlikely. There had been a possessiveness in Dominique's manner, but very little of the tenderness that Lissa associated instinctively with a long and faithful love. She pondered the problem while she quickly showered and changed into a navy pleated skirt and a matching blouse with full sleeves and a deep pointed collar at its high buttoning neck.

The two girls lunched alone. Madame Barrat, who served them explained that Monsieur le Comte and Monsieur Paul were out on the estate, and that Mademoiselle Vaumont had accompanied the two older women on their sightseeing trip.

'Oho!' Anne-Marie glanced mischievously at Lissa. 'Paul isn't very attentive for a new fiancé. You will have to take him in hand, Lissa.'

Lissa smiled briefly. 'I think he would have been very bored by this morning's activities,' she said. 'And this afternoon I must see if Maggie has left any work for me. I mustn't forget I'm her secretary first and fore-most, and not on vacation.'

Anne-Marie spread out her hands and looked ex-pressively at the ceiling.

'Grand'mère always said the English were not a demonstrative race. *C'est vrai, n'est-ce pas?*' she mur-mured.

Lissa laughed and went off to the library. As she suspected, there was a sheaf of closely written pages lying near the typewriter, so she got down to work straight away. She had been absorbed in her task for just over an hour when the sound of the door opening caused her to swing round from the typewriter. She was expecting Maggie, back from her outing, but in-stead Raoul de Gue was standing, watching her.

Lissa immediately felt vulnerable, and rose to her feet a little jerkily.

'Good afternoon, *monsieur*,' she said, her voice giv-ing a slight betraying quiver. He inclined his head courteously, and continued to look at her. The silence seemed to go on endlessly and Lissa felt her unsteady heartbeats must be clearly audible across the room.

'Why wouldn't you open your door to me last night?' he asked eventually.

Lissa controlled a gasp. 'I would have thought the answer to that would have been obvious, particularly to you, *monsieur*.'

'Indeed?' He raised his eyebrows coldly. 'I hope you are not insinuating that I would have been guilty of attempting to seduce someone who was a guest under my roof.'

'I am not able to say, *monsieur*, precisely what you would be capable of,' Lissa said breathlessly. 'How-ever, knowing your previous opinion of me, allowing you into my bedroom is the last thing I would do.'

'In spite of the fact that I made it clear that I had

something of great urgency to say to you.'

'Nothing that cannot be said here and now.' Lissa clenched her hands into fists in an attempt to stop them trembling. 'I suppose you are angry that I—deceived you over Paul.'

'You did not deceive me, Lissa. I suppose I may call you that sometimes, as you are to be my *belle-sœur*. Nor am I angry. My feelings at this moment, I should say, are mixed.'

He came away from the door and moved towards her. Instinctively, she backed away a few paces. He halted, watching her speculatively, then stepped forward again. Lissa, by now feeling incredibly foolish, retreated again and found herself literally with her back to the wall. She could move no further. Moreover, she had got herself into a corner, and her escape was blocked on one side by a wall of books.

Raoul de Gue moved forward unhurriedly until he was standing less than a foot in front of her. He leaned forward slightly and put one hand on the wall on her other side so that she was completely hemmed in, and stood in silence looking down into her face.

Lissa stood motionless, hardly daring to breathe. She felt devastated by her emotional confusion, as every inch of her body clamoured for his touch. Why had she let Paul talk her into this ridiculous situation? she wondered wildly. She wanted to cry the truth aloud to Raoul, to tell him she wanted him, no matter what the consequences might be.

Raoul stroked her cheek in the lightest of caresses with his free hand, then let his fingers trace the tender line of her jaw and throat. He paused for a moment, and then, still without hurry, undid the top two buttons of her blouse.

'This prim buttoned-up look does not at all become you, as I have good reason to recall,' he said coolly.

Lissa swung up her hand to slap his face, but he caught her wrist easily in the cramped space and held it.

'I do not advise it,' he drawled. 'I might be forced to retaliate in a way you would not like.'

'And you wondered,' she said slowly, 'why I would not open my door.'

'And I am also wondering why you ran away from me just now like a silly child. What do you imagine I would do to you here in my own library at this hour of the day—even if you were not engaged to my brother?' He released her and stepped back.

Lissa rubbed her wrist where the marks of his fingers still showed. Her throat felt dry and painful. Almost whispering, she said, 'What did you wish to say to me—last night, *monsieur*?'

He shook his head, smiling a little. 'In the cold light of day, I find it is no longer quite so urgent, or indeed so relevant.'

'Please go, then,' she said, staring at the floor. 'Please leave me alone.'

'As you wish.' He turned as if to leave, then suddenly swung back. 'Allow me to present my felicitations on your betrothal,' he said harshly. He pulled her into his arms, his hands hard in the small of her back, almost grinding her body against his own, and for one endless moment his mouth took hers.

Then he was gone, moving to the door with that characteristic quick lithe stride. At the door, he paused.

'Remind me to return to you the family jewels,' he said, and went out.

Maggie listened in stunned silence as Lissa poured out the whole sorry tale to her from beginning to end that evening.

'When you decide to get yourself into a mess, you

don't do it by halves,' she said ruefully. 'My dear girl, whatever possessed you to do such a crazy thing? And don't put all the blame on to Paul either. It's that good-looking wretch of a brother that's behind all this.'

'You couldn't be more wrong,' Lissa said clearly. 'I've never hated anyone in my life as I do him.'

'I knew it!' Maggie moaned. She folded her arms and gazed resignedly at her goddaughter. 'Well, I suppose the best thing would be to pack and get back to London before Paul persuades you to add an extra touch of conviction by going through the actual marriage ceremony with him.'

'Oh, no!' Lissa burst out impulsively. She bit her lip. 'I mean—the book. It would spoil everything.'

'The book can take care of itself, which is more than can be said for you,' Maggie said grimly. 'But I admit I hadn't planned on going back so soon.' She looked heavily at Lissa. 'It's not going to be easy for you, though, over the next few weeks. And I feel badly about deceiving Madame de Gue. She's too nice for that. And as for protecting her for her health's sake, I think this business is more likely to give her a heart attack when it all comes out, as it's bound to eventually.'

'I know,' Lissa sighed miserably. 'But at the time I only thought...'

'How you could get back at Raoul de Gue in one easy lesson,' Maggie said soothingly. 'Very understandable, my love, but not very sensible. Anyway, you won't have to face him again for a while. He's gone back to Paris and taken that sour-faced Dominique with him, so there'll be no need to taste your food for poison for a few days at least.'

'Taken Dominique?' Lissa repeated. There was an icy feeling in the pit of her stomach. She recalled with appalling clarity Paul's exultant remark that if Raoul still wanted the merger, he would have to do the honours himself. She made herself smile. 'He hasn't wasted much time!'

'I doubt if either of them are the type to let the grass grow under their feet,' Maggie said drily. 'Oh, Lissa, what have you done?'

It was a question that Lissa was asking herself more and more as the days lengthened into weeks. The book was going well, and she was glad of the constant demands on her time and energy that stopped her from too much self-analysis of her feelings and motives. Much of her spare time was spent working in the walled garden, which had soon lost its neglected appearance. But she worked there alone now, because Anne-Marie had also returned to her work in Paris.

As the days went on, Lissa found that her relationship with Paul was getting easier too, principally because he made no attempt to force it on to a more lover-like footing. He seemed content with the bargain they had made, but he would not agree to end it as Lissa had hoped, once Dominique was out of the way.

'Not until she is safely engaged herself,' he said one morning as they rode together by the river. Her new role as his fiancée had given her the freedom of the stables as well as the house and grounds, and Lissa would not have been human if she had not taken full advantage of it.

'But when will that be?' Lissa asked hopelessly.

Paul grinned, 'Not too long now, *chérie*, if I know Raoul.'

'Are you so certain that he will marry her?' Lissa ducked low in the saddle to avoid an overhanging branch and was glad of an excuse for her flushed face as she straightened.

'Of course. Nothing means more to Raoul than

Fontaines—unless of course it's the family honour,' Paul explained. 'No sacrifice is too much to ask—but for him, not for me.'

'Doesn't love come into it?'

'Not with Raoul,' he said. 'Certainly not since Victoire . . .' He shrugged almost regretfully.

He must have loved her very much, Lissa thought with a swift pang. She let her horse canter ahead. This was not a line of conversation she wished to pursue.

And then there was Françoise. Ever since the child had learned of the supposed engagement, there had been a shy welcome in her eyes each time she met Lissa. Usually she was in the charge of Mademoiselle Firaud, a drab young woman who peered at the world through unbecoming spectacles.

Surely the child would be happier at school? It was such an isolated existence for her at the Chateau, Lissa thought.

One day she ventured to raise the subject with the Comtesse, who was sitting with her embroidery on the terrace. So far Lissa had managed to evade any real exchange of confidences with her, and Madame had not pressed the point. She treated Lissa warmly and appeared quite content to let any relationship between them develop at its own pace. Lissa was half expecting a rebuff, but to her surprise Madame seized eagerly on her words.

'You are right, *ma chère*, but how to convince Raoul?' She sighed. 'He has laid down his own rules for the child's upbringing and I must not interfere, it seems. But it is hard. At Anne-Marie's old school, the good sisters would welcome and cherish the child. And she needs playmates of her own age.' Madame sighed again. 'And her clothes, *ma mie*! Even they are picked by Mademoiselle, who is worthy, I am sure, but altogether lacking in *chic*.' And she made a graceful gesture.

Lissa was bound to agree. She longed to take the little girl in hand, to dress her in jeans and run with her through the woods that surrounded the Chateau, letting her get dirty and untidy for once. She wanted to take her swimming in the deep pool below the St Denis bridge, where the village children splashed and played and sunned themselves on the rocks. Mademoiselle Firaud, it seemed, did not care over-much for fresh air and the sun brought on her frequently recurring headaches.

It was one of these headaches that finally gave Lissa her chance. She came running down the stairs late one afternoon on her way to the garden and found Françoise crouched on the bottom step, crying.

'What is it, *chérie*?' Lissa cradled the small body protectively.

'Mademoiselle promised we would go to the village today, but now she says she is *trop malade* and has gone to lie on her-bed.' Françoise sniffed, scrubbing at her eyes with a damp ball of a handkerchief. '*C'est toujours la même chose.* It is too hot or too far, or the heat makes her feel ill.' And the sobs broke out afresh.

There was an echo of many similar disappointments in the child's voice, Lissa recognised. She stood up briskly, pulling Françoise to her feet.

'Well, I wouldn't mind a walk to the village for a change,' she said, smiling. 'But I don't want to take a tear-stained face with me. Run along and wash it while I change out of these jeans, and I'll see you here in ten minutes.'

Françoise's piquant little face was suddenly alight. She pulled free and was gone, leaving Lissa to make her way more slowly back to her room to change into a

104

cool white sleeveless dress.

She had been looking forward to her time in the garden and the thought of a long hot walk down the steep hill to the village and back was not particularly enthralling.

'I'm behaving as a good aunt should,' she told herself drily, combing her soft fall of hair before the mirror.

But the child did not need an aunt. She needed mothering. Surely Raoul de Gue was aware of this? Perhaps even at this moment he was making plans for marriage, to give the child a mother she so badly needed. But would Dominique fill this particular role as well as all the others she would be called on to play as mistress of the Chateau and wife of its master?

Lissa dropped the comb back on the dressing table, conscious that her hand was trembling. Because she had only seen an unpleasant antagonistic side to Dominique, it did not mean that the girl was not possessed of other attributes that a man like Raoul de Gue would find distinctly alluring. Dominique was good-looking, and if her mouth was sulky, it was also sensual, with its full, pouting lower lip.

Paul had said love would not come into such a marriage, but Lissa thought bleakly that passion was a very different matter. The Comte would expect more than a mere business arrangement. And as for Dominique, Lissa found her attitude difficult to fathom. She had, it seemed, wanted Paul openly and without evasion. Now, equally openly, she had transferred her attentions to Raoul. It was incredible, Lissa thought, and unwanted and unbidden the question forced itself upon her teeming mind—'How could Raoul be only second-best to any woman?'

Françoise chattered gaily as they descended the winding road to St Denis. Lissa was glad of her prattle. It kept thoughts at bay that she did not wish to be confronted with, and she tried to respond to the child with equal gaiety.

It was very hot, and the loose stones underfoot pressed through the soles of her sandals, making her wriggle her toes uncomfortably. Perhaps Mademoiselle Firaud's frequent headaches were understandable after all, she decided wryly, pausing to dislodge one flint that had actually wedged itself under her heel.

She soon discovered that Françoise's wish to go to the village was not a simple desire for exercise. There was a confectioner's shop which sold sweets and ice cream, and Lissa guessed that a visit to this establishment was generally a highlight of the trip.

As they approached the bridge, Lissa saw that there were the usual children playing nearby, and was surprised to feel Françoise's hand steal into hers. Glancing down at the child's face, suddenly robbed of its mobility as she walked along silently with downcast eyes, Lissa realised that Françoise was desperately shy and awkward with the other children.

She noted too that they had stopped playing and were watching Françoise walk past almost with an air of resentment. As she and Françoise drew level, one of the children said something in a low voice, and the whole group laughed. There was an unkind note in the laughter, and Lissa saw Françoise bite her lower lip to stop it trembling.

'Do you know the girl—the one who spoke?' Lissa asked.

'She is Yvette Monceaux. Her father is the owner of the *épicerie*.' Françoise's voice was stilted.

Glancing back over her shoulder, Lissa saw that the children were still staring after them. One of them, a fair girl, leaned over and spoke to the Monceaux child, who frowned and shrugged before turning away to resume her skipping game with two others.

'Is Yvette older than you?'

'By a year, *mademoiselle*.' Lissa felt the small hand gently withdrawn from her own, just as she had felt the child retreat within herself. But why? Although she badly wanted to get to the bottom of the unpleasant little incident, Lissa decided it would be politic to let the matter drop for the time being. All the joyousness had gone out of Françoise's step, and she still looked close to tears.

'Here are the houses at last,' Lissa remarked. 'What pretty colours they are, and how nice some of the window-boxes look. If you had a window-box, what flowers would you grow in it, I wonder?'

'I do not know many flowers,' Françoise said doubtfully.

'Then your education has been sadly neglected,' Lissa said cheerfully. 'Particularly when your own great-grandmother has made such a lovely garden at the chateau. Don't you ever go there to play?'

'*Non.*' Françoise shook her head, and Lissa was glad to see she looked less wan. 'Pierre says that flower gardens are English and mad, and waste soil that could be used for growing good vegetables.'

A typically French point of view from the Chateau's head gardener, and a possible reason for all the past neglect, Lissa thought ruefully.

'Yet he keeps the gardens at the Chateau beauti fully,' she said.

'*Mais naturellement.* Papa would not employ him if he did not,' Françoise said practically, and Lissa was forced to laugh.

They spent a pleasant half hour in the village square. Françoise led Lissa from shop to shop, all her former vitality restored. Unlike some of their children, the village tradespeople appeared to treat her with warmth and affection, Lissa thought, feeling heartened.

When she had supervised the purchase of the biggest ice cream that Monsieur Durand had to sell, Lissa felt she deserved some refreshment on her own account. She eased the cuffed neckline of her dress away from the stickiness of her throat and gazed longingly across the square to the café where the proprietor had set the inevitable small tables on the pavement outside in the shade of tall umbrellas. A cup of tea would be more than welcome, but there would be small hope of that, she knew.

She decided instead on fresh lemonade with ice in it if possible, and set off across the square with Françoise skipping beside her in silent and rather sticky bliss.

Monsieur Archard brought her drink himself and paused to ask if she was enjoying her stay at the chateau. Lissa was aware that every detail of her dress and appearance had been closely studied by everyone they had encountered, and guessed unhappily that news of her so-called engagement had spread like wildfire. Paul had a lot to answer for in a great many ways, she thought angrily, as she pretended English incomprehension to Monsieur's smiling questions.

Her suspicions were soon confirmed by Françoise when Monsieur's plump figure had disappeared back into the café.

'Everyone wonders when you are going to marry *mon oncle*,' she said candidly, gazing at Lissa over the top of her ice cream. 'When there is a wedding in our family, there is a dance here at the square as well as the ball at the Chateau, and at midnight all the guests come down to the village here and join in the dancing. It happened when Papa married Maman. Uncle Paul told me all about it, and how everyone drank champagne and laughed and was happy. Soon it will be your turn, *mademoiselle*.'

'That being the case,' Lissa smiled at her, 'don't you think you could find something a little more friendly to call me than Mademoiselle?'

'*Ma tante*?' Françoise ventured, putting her head a little on one side.

Lissa felt a sudden flush of embarrassment. 'Well, it's a little too soon for that, perhaps. I wouldn't mind if you called me by my Christian name.'

'Lissa.' Françoise gazed at her, obviously startled. 'But Mademoiselle Firaud would say that was not *convenable*.'

'Well, with all due respect, I think we can leave Mademoiselle and her opinions out of this,' Lissa said, firmly. 'So it's settled, then.'

'*Certainement*—Lissa,' smiled Françoise, her look of mischief bringing her close to real prettiness.

Sitting there in the shade of the umbrella, listening idly to Françoise as she pointed out the various village notables as they went about their business, Lissa failed utterly to notice the sleek dark red sports car easing its way towards them between a cyclist and a knot of gossiping women. Françoise saw it, however, and was on her feet in an instant, gleefully waving.

'Papa, Papa! *Nous sommes ici*!'

Lissa's heart froze as she recognised the elegant dark figure at the wheel and realised that he had seen them and that he was not alone. Dominique was in the passenger seat.

The car whispered to a halt at the kerb a few feet away and Raoul de Gue got out slowly. He was wearing dark glasses so his expression was unreadable as Françoise ran over to him, but Lissa noticed that he quietly disengaged himself from the child's ecstatic grip after a brief greeting.

'So you have a new companion on your excursions,' he remarked slowly. He did not seem annoyed, but rather slightly amused, and Lissa felt her tension increasing. She made to stand up, instinctively reaching for her handbag which lay on the table near her half-finished glass of lemonade. Her arm caught the tumbler and the remains of the liquid splashed on to her dress. With a little exclamation she fell back on to the seat, pulling open the clasp of her bag to get a tissue. But before she could find one, an immaculately folded handkerchief was dropped into her lap. Furious with herself for her clumsiness and lack of poise, she muttered a brief word of thanks and devoted her attention to her stained skirt. Her feeling of awkwardness was not dispelled by his reaching down and touching one of the folds.

'It will wash?' he asked.

'Very easily,' Lissa returned a little unsteadily. Of course, he would be interested in the fabric and its qualities.

'I am relieved to hear it. I wouldn't want to be responsible for ruining any more of your wardrobe,' he said, coolly straightening.

'Have I to wait here all afternoon?' Dominique's voice suddenly demanded from the car. Raoul strolled across and opened the passenger door.

'Certainly not, *ma chère*. We will all sit and drink lemonade and then I will drive Françoise and Mademoiselle Fairfax back to the Chateau. I imagine the walk down was quite sufficient,' he added, directing a glance at Lissa's flimsy white sandals.

Dominique got out of the car with obvious ill grace.

'And what would they have done if we hadn't arrived?' she demanded.

'The question does not arise.' Raoul held a chair for her with smiling courtesy and signalled to the hover-

110

ing Monsieur Archard.

After sending one rather derisive look at her dress, Dominique apparently preferred to pretend that Lissa was not there. She turned to Françoise with vivacity, firing a quick flood of questions that Lissa was sure were mainly concerned with the schoolroom and Mademoiselle Firaud. Françoise answered dutifully, but Lissa could see that her heart was not in it, and was amused to see the child trying valiantly to repress a yawn as Dominique continued to press questions on her progress in mathematics.

Lissa did not want another glass of lemonade, but she did not know how to refuse it or the lift back to the Chateau without seeming churlish. With a start, she realised that in her abstraction she had been about to put Raoul de Gue's handkerchief in her bag, and saw him smile faintly as he reached across to take it from her. It was that smile that decided her. She would walk back to the Chateau if it killed her! She wanted no favours from him, a man who thought she would melt at his slightest glance, even though the thought of that hill and the heat and stones made her wince in advance.

She took the lemonade with a cold 'Merci' when it came, and went on staring across the square as if her life depended on it.

'It is dedicated to the Assumption of the Blessed Virgin,' Raoul's voice said in her ear, and she jumped.

'What is?'

'The church, in which you seem to be taking such an absorbing interest.' He had lit a Gauloise and was leaning back on his chair, watching her from behind those enigmatic dark glasses.

'I was not aware of it,' she said coldly.

'You gave the impression that you were memorising every stone,' he returned. 'No doubt you were lost in dreams of the happy days when you will stand before its altar as Paul's bride.'

'No doubt,' said Lissa, nettled, and saw him smile again.

'I wouldn't bank too much on dreams of that nature,' he told her too softly for the others to hear, and she tensed.

'Are you threatening me, Monsieur le Comte?'

'*Au contraire*. Consider it more in the light of a friendly warning.'

'Indeed?' Lissa in spite of her growing rage, was also careful to keep her voice down. 'Well, I'm sorry, *monsieur*, but I don't believe that friendship is possible between us.'

'You could well be right.' He studied the burning tip of his cigarette.

'I'm glad we agree on that at least. So perhaps you will also agree to stop—sniping all the time at my relationship with Paul.'

'I am sorry if that is how you regard my natural interest in your little affair,' he said. 'I cannot promise to relax it, however. Too much, you see, depends on the outcome for that.' He smiled sardonically as he saw her glance uncertainly at Dominique. 'Precisely.'

'I'm sorry too.' Lissa drained what was left in her glass and set the tumbler down a little breahtlessly. 'You're hundreds of years out of date, you know. Autocrats of your type died out in the Revolution, or should have done. One thing is certain—neither Paul nor I are going to submit to being bullied by you. We have our own lives to lead. And—and I would prefer to get back to the Chateau under my own steam, thank you,' she ended a little lamely.

'Fortunately that won't be necessary,' he said smoothly, lifting his hand in a casual greeting. Turning in her chair, Lissa saw Paul walking along the

112

pavement towards them. 'In the nick of time, *mon brave*. Your lovely fiancée has just been defending you like an angry tigress protecting her cub.'

'Oh?' Paul looked hot and cross. 'Well, I've just left another angry tigress up at the Chateau. I wish you'd told Mademoiselle Firaud that you were bringing Françoise down here with you, Lissa. She's convinced the child has been kidnapped at the very least. Fortunately Madame Barrat saw you leave and calmed her down before she started agitating Maman.'

'Oh!' Lissa's already burning cheeks glowed afresh with humiliation. 'I thought—I assumed that Françoise had told her ...' She looked at the little girl, who sat looking the picture of guilt.

'Hardly,' Raoul de Gue drawled. 'I suspect Françoise knew she would not get permission for the treat and decided to bypass Mademoiselle altogether.' He rose with the restrained muscular grace that characterised his every move. 'Come, Françoise. We will discuss the matter and your apology to Mademoiselle in the car, *hein*? Paul, you will drive Mademoiselle Fairfax?'

Lissa turned away and began to walk along the pavement. She was embarrassed and annoyed that her wish to give a child pleasure had turned out like this. She had been made to feel both interfering and thoughtless, and the fact that Dominique had been a gloating witness didn't help in the slightest.

Paul caught up with her. 'You'll give yourself a headache, *chérie*, if you charge about in the heat like this.' He looked at her with concern. 'Are you all right, Lissa?'

Lissa sighed. 'I suppose so. I didn't realise Françoise wasn't supposed to leave the Chateau without permission.'

Paul looked uncomfortable. 'In the old days, it did not seem to matter. And there is no harm done as she was with you, but she is a rich man's daughter, and there is always a certain amount of danger. But Mademoiselle tends to panic when Françoise isn't under her eye. And this afternoon, she should have been in the schoolroom with her embroidery.' He paused and looked at her curiously. 'What have you been saying to Raoul? What did he mean about your defending me?'

'It doesn't matter,' Lissa said wearily. 'He was just being unpleasant about our supposed engagement. Don't let's talk about it. I've had about as much as I can stand today.'

As Paul's estate car wound its way up the hill, the sports car overtook it easily. Paul sounded his horn and shook his fist in mock menace, while his brother responded with a casual wave.

'I've never known Raoul spend so much time at the Chateau as he has this month,' said Paul, as they followed the other car through the gates. 'I wish I knew why.' He looked worriedly at Lissa. 'You'll keep your word, *chérie*. You won't let him know that our engagement is a sham until he and Dominique are *fiancés*?'

'No, I won't tell him,' Lissa promised wanly. And even her silently expressed conviction that Raoul and Dominique deserved each other brought her no comfort.

## CHAPTER SEVEN

LISSA's dreams were troubled that night and she slept only fitfully. It was not surprising, therefore, that she woke with a slight headache, and a general disinclination to go downstairs and face the situation.

Dinner, the previous evening, had been an awkward meal full of constrained silences. Even Dominique had not made her usual attempt to monopolise the conversation, but had confined herself to intimately low-voiced exchanges with Raoul de Gue.

And Paul had decided the time was ripe for a little lover-like behaviour on his own behalf, Lissa recalled angrily. She had been forced, in public, to play along with this, concealing her rising irritation, largely for the sake of Madame de Gue, who seemed pleased that this strange courtship by her younger son was being conducted along conventional lines at last.

Lissa supposed that had she been in love with Paul, his attentions would have been the summit of her wildest dreams. As it was, the way he had leaned over her, his cheek brushing her hair to fill her wine glass or his hand cupping hers as he lit her cigarette had almost stifled her. And when he had sat beside her on the brocaded sofa in the salon so close that he seemed almost moulded to her side, it was all Lissa could do not to push him away.

The only person who seemed unaware of the undercurrents had been Maggie, who had excused herself immediately the meal was over to re-immerse herself in the de Gue family papers. She was so preoccupied with them, and the diary in particular, that Lissa had decided not to bother her at this time with her personal doubts and troubles. She knew her godmother had reached a particular phase in her creative process, which was extremely sensitive, and that she needed no outside disturbances. Besides, Lissa realised ruefully, Maggie's probable reaction would be that she had brought all her problems on herself. Lissa felt that this was only partly true. She argued with herself that she had been forced into her present invidious position by the vile, contemptible behaviour of Raoul de Gue who seemed to think he had the right to play the *grand seigneur* over the destiny of everyone he came across.

What she did not choose to examine too closely was her own incredibly over-heated reaction to him, quite apart from the undeniable physical onslaught he had made on her senses.

She sat up in bed with a groan, pushing the tumbled hair off her damp forehead. She had arranged to meet Paul for their usual morning ride in a very short while, she realised as she consulted her wristwatch. It would do her good to get away from the brooding atmosphere of the Chateau for a while, and she could also, she thought, lay down some strict guidelines for Paul on their future relationship while she remained in France. They had a bargain after all, no matter how distasteful it might have become.

After a quick shower, she hurriedly dressed in her levis and a black high-necked jumper and pulled on knee-length boots before making her way downstairs and out to the stables through the kitchen quarters as she had inadvertently done on her first day.

But to her dismay, a *tête-à-tête* with Paul was to be out of the question, it seemed. Paul himself, with a face like thunder, was standing by one of the stalls, tapping his riding crop against his boot, and watching Raoul helping Dominique to mount Verité, the little mare that Lissa usually rode on their excursions. The groom, Jean-Louis, stood holding the bridle of Mistral for the Comte and Lissa saw that Atalante, a young mare she had not tried before, had been saddled for her.

For a moment she hesitated, wondering if she could retreat to the Chateau without being seen, and plead slight indisposition later, but Paul had already noticed her and was striding across the courtyard.

'There you are, *chérie*,' he said loudly. 'You don't mind if we have company for once, do you?'

Lissa felt embarrassed, especially when she encountered a slightly mocking smile from the Comte, as he leaned forward in his saddle to smooth Mistral's neck.

'It isn't for me to mind,' she said sharply, needled by that smile. 'They are your brother's horses, after all, and he may ride them whenever he wishes.'

It was a graceless little speech and she wished it unsaid almost at once. Paul's scowl deepened, but he remained silent, and Lissa pretended to occupy herself in tightening Atalante's girth.

'Which way shall we go, Raoul?' Dominique asked. She was looking extremely chic as usual in a silk shirt and superbly cut riding breeches.

'Down by the river—that's the way you usually go, isn't it, Paul?' Raoul turned to his brother, who had also mounted by this time.

An imp of perversity awoke in Lissa. This party was none of her choosing, she thought. She could at least pick her own route for her morning ride.

She kept her head bent and went on fiddling with the girth which was now adjusted to her satisfaction.

'*Allons*, Lissa. *Dépêches-toi!*' Paul called impatiently.

'My stirrup's a little too long. I'll catch you up,' she called back, and smiled to herself as she saw the Comte with Paul and Dominique close behind him urge their horses to a trot out of the yard.

She waited until the sound of hooves had died away and glanced round. But Jean-Louis had disappeared into one of the stalls and would not be around, Lissa reasoned, to point out to her that she was going in the wrong direction.

Outside the gates, a narrow rather dusty track followed the high wall of the Chateau grounds downwards and out of sight round a slight bend. Lissa turned Atalante's head in the other direction and coaxed the mare, who seemed nervous after the placid Verité, up the track towards the woodland that crowned the slopes at the back of the Chateau.

She felt like a child playing truant as the trees closed round her, and wondered if her absence had been noticed yet. She speculated mischievously on which of the trio would be the most angry at her defection—Raoul and Dominique, who would obviously want to be alone—or Paul, who for the first time in his life probably would find himself the third member of a party in which two was the only company.

Meanwhile, the track led into the woodland, becoming a broad grassy bridle path, and just the place to take the fidgets out of Atalante, Lissa decided as she put the mare into a controlled canter, and then, encouraged by the animal's disciplined response, into a gallop.

Up above the arching trees, the sun gleamed in dappled splendour through the leaves, and below her, on her left, Lissa saw the glint of water and realised that she too was following the river, although at a much greater height than the others.

She slowed Atalante gradually until they were at a walking pace again. A few strands of hair had worked loose from the black velvet ribbon that held them at the nape of her neck, and she twisted the reins loosely round her wrist as she made the adjustment.

It was then that she heard the unmistakable sound of hoofbeats coming along the track from the direction she had just come from.

'Oh, no!' Lissa groaned aloud, giving her ribbon an extra vicious jerk. She supposed philosophically it was inevitable that Paul should come to search for her, acting out his role of the devoted fiancé. And undoubtedly he would have had some pretty strong hints from the other two to contend with as well. Resignedly she reined Atalante in to the side of the track and waited for him to come up with her, round the slight curve in the ride.

But it was not Paul's thickset grey who swung into view out of the screening trees. It was the bay, Mistral, and there was no mistaking the tall dark figure who rode as if he and his handsome mount were one, moulded together into a devastating partnership of grace and muscle that threatened to ride her down.

Lissa panicked. Nothing—nothing in this world was going to prevail on her to be alone with him again. She gave Atalante a sharp dig with her heels and the surprised mare responded with a bounding start which nearly unseated her.

He called her name and there was no mistaking the threatening note in his voice.

'Go to hell!' she shouted back recklessly, and crouched low over Atalante's neck, urging her along with her heels.

The wind whistled past and somewhere, in the distance at first, but growing steadily nearer, there was a low roaring noise that bore no relation to anything she could see, or even to the relentless hooves that already seemed to be gaining on her.

Sweat poured down her forehead, and trickled into her eyes, and she shook her head impatiently, not daring to relax sufficiently to wipe it away. Now she had taken to flight, all that seemed important was that she should win—get far enough away to hide in the trees, and hope that Raoul would get tired of looking for her eventually.

There was a sharp bend just ahead, she realised thankfully, her pulses pounding almost uncontrollably and her breath coming in shuddering gasps. Once round it, she would be out of sight for precious seconds.

The roaring was louder now, or was it merely the wind in her ears and her own laboured breathing that she heard? And as she and Atalante hurtled round the bend, she saw too late the torrent of white water hurtling down from a sheer wall of grey stone and how the ground fell away almost at their feet into a sloping ravine where jagged rocks peered malevolently out of the foaming water.

She heard herself cry out, and Atalante neighed furiously, rearing up in terror as her hooves slipped on the muddy bank. Then rocks, sky and water swung round her in one gigantic terrifying parabola as she fell.

It was an aching, uncertain world that she eventually opened her eyes on. She gazed round in bewilderment, conscious that her side felt sore and bruised and that her clothes were damp and streaked with mud. Her face, too, felt stiff and when she lifted a hand gingerly to investigate, it too came away coated in mud. And as tears of mingled pain and self-pity began to gather in her eyes, Raoul de Gue came climbing up the bank from the ravine. He was holding in his hand the crimson neckerchief he had been wearing in the open neck of his shirt, and Lissa could see that it was dripping wet.

Hastily she closed her eyes, and pretended to be still unconscious. She felt altogether too jarred, physically and emotionally, for a confrontation with him. She could sense that he was standing over her, looking down. There was that faint *frisson* along all her nerve endings that he never failed to inspire, damn him.

She risked an upward glance at him through her lashes and saw him dark against the sun. She realised helplessly that he was coming closer and shut her eyes again determinedly. She guessed rather than saw he was kneeling beside her. She could feel the warmth of him as he leaned over her. The sharp tang of his cologne was in her nostrils and she breathed it helplessly, knowing that his face could only be inches from her own.

He sighed, and she tensed involuntarily, aware that once more she was at his mercy through her own folly.

'*Alors, ma belle dormante,* it is time you awoke,' he murmured, and Lissa, in spite of herself, felt her breathing quicken as her lips parted awaiting his.

Instead a cold stream of water showered down on her as he wrung his neckerchief over her face and throat, and Lissa sat up gasping and shaking herself furiously.

'You ... brute! You've almost drowned me!'

Raoul sat back on his heels watching her with narrowed eyes.

'A miraculous recovery, *mademoiselle*. I felicitate you. You did indeed almost drown, but that was none of my doing.'

'I did?' Lissa had found some crumpled tissues in the pocket of her jeans and was trying to wipe her face. There was a grim note in his voice which gave her pause. She looked at him wide-eyed. 'Did I really fall ... in there?'

'Very nearly. Fortunately some bushes broke your fall and I was able to drag you back before they gave way.' His mouth was set and his eyes glinted ominously. 'Now you will have the goodness to explain to me what this little cross-country race was all about, and why you felt it necessary to risk your neck and that of an expensive animal which does not belong to you. The first, I cannot prevent, if you are determined. The second, I can and will.'

'Oh, Atalante!' Lissa struggled to a sitting position and stared around, wincing a little. She saw with relief that the mare was tied safely to a nearby tree and that both she and Mistral were quietly cropping the grass.

'Oh, Atalante,' he mimicked savagely, and she shrank at the sudden blaze of anger in his face. 'How dared you do it! You heard me shout to you. I was trying to warn you. We all know this path and are prepared for the waterfall. You knew nothing of it— Paul said that he had never brought you this way, and yet you rode as if all the devils in hell were after you.'

'Perhaps I thought they were,' Lissa threw back at him, and could have bitten out her tongue as soon as the words were uttered. He looked down at her, and in that one glance Lissa saw how his ancestors, proud lords of an *ancien régime* that took what they wanted from unruly vassals, would have reacted to such an insult and from a woman.

'So I am a devil,' he said softly. 'Why then ... welcome to my hell.'

Her mouth tightly closed against his insistence, she fought him breathlessly, until he savagely clamped his hand around her slender wrists and thrust them behind her back, pushing her down upon the grass. She cried out then partly in pain, and partly in protest at the insolent toll his mouth was taking of hers at last ... as if he would teach her a lesson in sensuality that she would remember until the end of her days.

Lying beneath his hard body, Lissa felt all her defences carefully constructed against him, all her anger and resentment slowly crumbling under sharper and more eloquent needs. All the lighthearted flirtations in the past had not prepared her for this desperate wanting, this longing to be drawn ever closer to him into the final consummation of passion.

He unfastened the buttons of his shirt, dragging the soft wool of her sweater aside so that his skin touched hers. It went through Lissa like an electric shock, and she shivered uncontrollably as he bent to kiss her again. And as he bent, he smiled and his grip on her wrists slackened, as though he was acknowledging the imminence of her complete surrender.

And in that moment Lissa broke the sensually drugged spell that was enfolding her. She had seen that smile and its implicit triumph.

That was all it was to him—a sordid little victory in his war of domination with Paul. She thrust him away from her with both hands, rolling over swiftly in spite of her bruises so that she was away from him. She would not let him see how seriously she had taken what had just passed between them. He would not have the satisfaction of knowing how nearly she had been completely his.

She tried to laugh, and was amazed at the lighthearted sound from a throat that ached with tears she would not allow herself to shed.

'I think this has gone far enough—don't you, *monsieur*? I didn't know that you still operated the *droit du seigneur* in this day and age.'

She got to her feet, brushing mud and grass from her jeans in an attempt to disguise how her hands were trembling. Her pulse felt ragged and she was aware of a shaming desire to be violently sick.

She stared at the ground and waited, shaking, for the nauseated feeling to pass.

Raoul de Gue had also risen, but he made no move

to approach her. When eventually she raised her eyes to meet his, the contempt in his face was like a blow.

'You are mistaken, *mademoiselle*,' his voice cut her like a whip. 'The *droit du seigneur* was invariably reserved for virgins—on their wedding nights.'

She was going to slap him right across that dark, mocking face of his, except that the nauseated feeling had returned stronger than ever. As it was, she managed two wavering steps before the ground dipped and swayed, and she fainted away again, right at his feet.

'Well,' said Maggie. Her tone conveyed a wealth of inflections in that simple monosyllable, and Lissa, lying wanly against her pillows, winced.

The doctor had left only a few moments before. Her cuts and bruises had been attended to, as they were only minor, and a form of sedative had been prescribed.

'Mademoiselle has suffered a severe shock to her nerves,' he diagnosed. Mademoiselle did not argue the point.

Lissa knew she was about to be the recipient of one of her godmother's rare censures, now that they were alone—severe shock to the nerves, or not.

'I had a word with Madame today,' said Maggie in measured tones. 'She was speaking of your engagement to Paul and wondering when it would be *convenable* to make the announcement public and give a party in your honour.'

'Oh, no!' Lissa raised stricken eyes.

'Oh, yes,' said Maggie grimly. 'You can imagine how I felt. I had to bring in pressure of work and all sorts of things to put her off the scent.' She paused for a moment. 'And I did say as well that I felt that things were not quite right between you and Paul, and that perhaps anything official would be premature.'

'Oh.' Lissa digested this for a moment. 'What did she say?'

'She was extremely sorry, but not, I felt, unduly surprised. She had apparently begun to welcome the idea of you as a daughter-in-law. I can't imagine why,' Maggie said dauntingly.

'Neither can I.' Lissa rolled over in bed, tears pricking at her eyelids.

'And crying won't help.' Maggie sat down on the edge of the bed and took her hand. 'While we're about it I would like an explanation of this morning's exhibition. Madame and I had just finished talking when Raoul de Gue came striding in carrying you in his arms. I thought you were dead at least.'

'I wish I was,' Lissa told her pillow.

'Nonsense,' said Maggie robustly. Her eyes concernedly surveyed the forlorn figure in bed. 'But seriously, dear, what made you take such an appalling risk? What could I have said to your parents if anything had happened to you?'

'I didn't realise there was a risk.' Lissa sat up slowly.

'No risk—in accepting a challenge from the Comte to a race over ground you didn't know? I thought the pair of you had more sense—and he far more sense of responsibility.'

Lissa put up a hand to her aching head. What was Maggie saying—that Raoul de Gue had taken the blame for what had happened? She felt bewildered. After his treatment of her, she had not believed it possible of him.

Maggie was continuing, 'I'm afraid he got a roasting for it from Madame. I've never seen her so upset. And then Paul and the dreadful Dominique arrived back, demanding to know what had happened. That was when I made a tactical withdrawal.' She leaned forward and looked closely at Lissa. 'Are you very shaken, ducky? You're very white. If I draw the curtains a little, could you sleep?'

Lissa murmured a subdued affirmative. Actually she did not feel in the least sleepy, but she felt a sudden urgent need to be alone.

When Maggie had gone, she closed her eyes and let the hot shamed tears begin to fall at last. Every moment with Raoul in the wood was recalled in all its bitter context. How could she so wantonly desire a man who so obviously despised her? she asked herself despairingly. Had she no pride at all where he was concerned? For no one else had her body known that sweet melting to oblivion. She groaned out loud, and pressed her knuckles hard against her teeth.

She tried to assemble her thoughts into some sort of coherent order. First of all she had to acknowledge that Raoul de Gue attracted her physically in a way that no other man ever had, and she fought away the treacherous afterthought—or ever would.

Secondly, her engagement to Paul must be ended. She could not have felt more guilty about Raoul's lovemaking if she had been truly Paul's fiancée, and bound to him in honour. No wonder Raoul held her in such contempt, she told herself. He had little enough reason to think well of her, even at their first meeting. The bitter truth was that she had never had sufficient control of herself to hold him at arm's length. Even Paul, whom she had once imagined she had loved a little, had teased her about her coldness.

Finally, she must get away from the Chateau as soon as she decently could. Maggie's book would soon be sufficiently advanced to permit a return to London, and Lissa felt that Maggie herself would not be too hard to persuade, now that she knew what the situation was.

Lissa smothered a sigh and reached listlessly for the

small box of capsules the doctor had left. Perhaps if she could sleep, she would feel more like sorting out the mess she had made for herself in some more positive and decisive way.

But it was a shallow, uneasy kind of sleep that eventually overtook her, with strange confused dreams. In one of them Raoul was standing by the bed and she was reaching out her hand to him desperately, begging him wordlessly for the comfort of his touch. But the tall dark figure seemed only to recede, the more she stretched towards him, and she felt the bitterness of tears sharp in her throat.

But in spite of the dreams, she did feel slightly more refreshed when she awoke some hours later, as though her over-emotional state had been purged away while she was unconscious.

She stretched languidly, aware that the sun was pouring in at the window through a gap in the curtains, and almost insensibly her spirits began to rise.

There was a tap on the door, and she called '*Entrez*', expecting Madame Barrat or one of the maids, but it was Françoise's piquant little face that peeped round the door at her, and she sat up immediately, smiling a welcome. Françoise advanced a little hesitantly into the room, and Lissa, with a suppressed smile, saw that she carried a book under her arm.

'I did not wake you?' the little girl asked anxiously as she came over to the bed, and Lissa shook her head reassuringly.

'I should be glad of some company,' she said. 'That looks a nice book. Did Papa give it to you?'

Françoise shook her head with that air of constraint Lissa had noticed before. 'Tante Anne-Marie brought it from Paris when she last visited here. Grand'mère says that Papa is too busy to concern himself with shopping for little girls.'

But surely every father indulged an only daughter, especially so tragically motherless a child as Françoise, Lissa thought uneasily. There was something very wrong here. She remembered Françoise's stillness in her father's presence and her almost shy overtures to him—as if they were strangers. And yet the French had a reputation for being devoted parents. It was a disturbing oddity in the household. Raoul was not a cold man, Lissa thought, flushing, so why then was his behaviour towards his only child so unemotional?

'Lissa?' Françoise stood biting her lip uncertainly, and Lissa put out her hand.

'Come and read to me,' she suggested, putting on a determinedly cheerful face, and the little girl responded with a smile like sunshine after rain, as she ran to curl up on the bed beside Lissa.

It was a book of French traditional fairy stories, lavishly illustrated, and Françoise's favourite was 'Cinderella'. Lissa was intrigued as the little girl read to learn that the fabled glass slipper of the English version was in fact made of fur in the original, and guessed that a mistake must have been made in translation. 'Ah, well, another illusion shattered,' she thought, grinning to herself.

When Françoise had finished the story, Lissa began to tell her of her own schooldays and of the pantomime version of that same 'Cinderella' they had once performed at Christmas.

'Were you Cinderella?' Françoise asked, putting up her hand to touch Lissa's fair hair.

Lissa grinned. 'No, I was one of the Ugly Sisters.'

'You are not ugly!' Françoise insisted indignantly.

Lissa smiled. 'Thanks for the vote of confidence,' she began, then paused as another knock came at the door, a firm authoritative tap this time, and Lissa tensed as Raoul de Gue walked into the room.

He was not looking at her, Lissa realised at once, but at the child curled up beside her.

'What are you doing here, Françoise?' he asked coldly. 'Why are you not with Mademoiselle Firaud?'

Françoise's lip trembled mutinously. 'I don't like being with her. She is always cross and complaining. I want to stay with Lissa.'

'That is not the point,' her father said, grimly. 'Mademoiselle Firaud is your teacher and at this time of day you should still be at your lessons. Run along at once. Besides, Mademoiselle Fairfax is not well and must rest, and you are being a nuisance to her.'

Lissa moved restlessly in denial, but Françoise was before her.

'I don't like having a *gouvernante*. When Lissa was a little girl she went to school where there were lots of children and she always had someone to play with. I have no one now,' she ended on a little sob.

Her father pointed inexorably to the door. 'Go.'

Françoise went, dragging her feet along the carpet. She looked utterly forlorn.

Lissa watched her go, then turned impulsively to Raoul. 'Please—don't be angry with her. It was my fault, I suppose, telling her about my own schooldays. I was so happy at school, you see, and she's so obviously unhappy.'

'She seemed content enough—before.'

'Before you came,' were the unspoken words, Lissa thought wildly. She said, 'But that's not enough, Raoul. A child of that age just content. She should be bubbling over with high spirits—every day should be an adventure. But look at her!'

'I do look at her, he said remotely.

'But what do you see?' Lissa leaned forward in the bed, regardless of her flimsy nightgown, her voice rising passionately. 'Just an extension of your own pride

and family tradition—or a living, breathing child—
your own child, Raoul, whom for some reason you
don't even seem to love.'

Her voice ended on a note of appeal, but she was
shockedly aware that she had gone too far and waited
for the thunderbolt to descend, as she met his blazing
dark eyes. But when he spoke his voice was icily quiet.

'Permit me to remind you, *mademoiselle*, that your
position in this family does not yet give you the right
to interfere in my affairs—especially in my private
relationships.'

There was an aching pause. Lissa said numbly, 'I'm
sorry.' But his tall figure was already at the door and
he did not turn or acknowledge that he had even
heard her apology.

She felt close to tears when she was alone, but even
the knowledge that she had been wrong to take Raoul
to task as she had could not suppress the fierce vein of
anger that possessed her when she thought of his chilly
treatment of his daughter. Perhaps it was grief for the
wife who had so suddenly been taken from him. Perhaps Françoise reminded him too poignantly of what
had been, Lissa thought despondently. It was not a
flight of fancy that she cared to pursue.

One thing was certain. She would not allow Raoul's
indifference to colour her own attitude to Françoise,
whom she found an enchanting child, but desperately
in need of constant attention and affection. It seemed
likely to Lissa that the child was starved of love, apart
from that brief daily contact with her grandmother in
the salon before dinner.

'If no one else bothers with her, then I will,' she
thought recklessly, pushing the disturbing question
about what would happen to the child when she was
no longer available to the back of her mind.

It was important, she felt, to start as she meant to go

on, and to show Françoise that her dismissal from her bedroom need not count too strongly with her.

Accordingly, the following afternoon, dressed in her jeans and matching shirt, she made her way with a little trepidation to the schoolroom to approach Mademoiselle Firaud.

Although it was a warm day, all the large windows were tightly closed, she noticed immediately, as she put her head round the door. Mademoiselle was sitting on one side of a small table, deep in a book, while Françoise, visibly drooping, was seated opposite her, a small and rather grubby piece of sewing in her hands.

Making her smile and voice as winning as possible, Lissa explained that she was about to do some weeding in the walled garden and would be delighted if Françoise could accompany her to give some assistance.

'It would be a valuable lesson in botany for her,' she added for good measure, noticing that Mademoiselle was frowning a little.

Françoise threw down her sewing and jumped up, almost hopping from one foot to another in her eagerness.

'I suppose there is no harm,' the governess said grudgingly at last. 'Please to be sure that *la petite* does not get overtired and does not take sunstroke, *mademoiselle*.'

Lissa promised to take special care, and she and Françoise left the stuffy room hand in hand.

Lissa spent an entertaining half an hour pointing out to Françoise, who tended at first to pull up anything and everything, the difference between plants and weeds. The little girl was quick to learn, however, and soon they had cleared the weeds out of one of the smaller beds in a shady corner of the garden.

Lissa sat back on her heels and regarded her handiwork.

'Not bad at all,' she said.

'I am a good gardener, me,' Françoise announced gleefully.

'Cheek!' Lissa picked up a small clump of grass and threw it at her playfully. Almost at once, a larger clump came whizzing back and scored a direct hit on Lissa's shoulder. Turning, she saw Françoise watching her with an almost terrified look of apprehension—anxious to know the reaction of her first bit of horse-play, Lissa thought with a wave of sympathy. She got up, rolling up her sleeves.

'Right, Mademoiselle de Gue,' she lowered her voice to a mock growl. 'Over my knee you go.'

Françoise jumped up squealing and fled. Lissa chased her round the paths, jumping over the smaller beds and dodging backwards and forwards around the jasmine arbour.

Françoise was shrieking with laughter. Her plaits had come undone from their prim coronet, and her face was flushed and smudged with dirt. She'll do, Lissa thought exultantly, and grabbed her as she tried to dodge across the newly cut lawn. Françoise collapsed on the grass with howls of glee as Lissa began tickling her.

Like a sudden icy blast, a voice from the gateway said scornfully, '*Quelle bêtise!*'

Looking up, Lissa found Dominique standing watching them, a palpable sneer marring her attractive face.

The laughter stopped abruptly and Françoise got to her feet and stood twisting her hands. Lissa too felt uncomfortable in her faded earth-stained jeans, especially compared with Dominique, who was resplendent in a cream silk trouser suit with a purple scarf at her neck.

'How long has this—romping been permitted?' Dominique asked coldly. 'Madame la Comtesse is looking for you, Françoise. I suggest you make yourself presentable before you go to her.'

Lissa felt that Madame's heart would be only gladdened by the sight of Françoise in her present state, but she was unwilling to have an open conflict in front of the child. Instead she gave Françoise a swift hug. 'Run along now, darling,' she said. 'And mind you scrub those hands!'

Françoise ran off obediently, and Lissa was left alone with Dominique. She felt at some kind of disadvantage and could have kicked herself for it. There was an elastic band in the pocket of her jeans and she scooped her dishevelled hair back into this as casually as she could under Dominique's contemptuous stare.

'I did not know you were still here, *mademoiselle*,' she said, trying to be pleasant.

'*Non?*' Dominique's tone conveyed a number of different inflections. A kind of triumphant smugness predominated. 'I notice you have lost no time in trying to make yourself one of the family, Mademoiselle Fairfax,' she continued. She took a step towards Lissa and her voice became loaded with malice. 'Well, do what you will, you will always be an interloper. There have been enough English brides at the Chateau. Why don't you take yourself off back to London where you belong?'

Lissa kept a tight rein on her temper.

'Not everyone regards me as an interloper,' she said. 'And I shall be part of the family if I marry Paul.'

She was immediately angry with herself for saying 'if' and not 'when', and Dominique's eyes gleamed at the slip.

'Do you really think Raoul will allow you to marry Paul?' she asked offensively. 'He knows the kind of woman you are.' She gave a little reminiscent laugh. 'Another Victoire in the family—that would have been too much!'

Lissa stood stunned under the attack. Another Victoire? she asked herself in bewilderment. What in the world was Dominique getting at?

Dominique came nearer still. Her lips glistened in the sunlight, as she moistened them with her tongue.

'And don't imagine you can gain favour with Raoul by making a fuss of Françoise,' she went on stridently. 'You are crazy if you think he cares for her. She's just a living reminder of the worst mistake he ever made.'

'His own child?' Lissa burst out, in spite of herself.

Dominique's laugh seemed to hammer back at her from the encircling walls of the garden.

'That's it exactly, you little fool. She isn't his child at all. Victoire told him so herself.'

Lissa stared at her for one horror-struck moment, then she was running past Dominique, her fingers pressed to her ears, out of the garden and back to the Chateau.

# CHAPTER EIGHT

LISSA's mind was in turmoil as she waited for Maggie in her room, prior to going down to dinner that evening. The thought of food was abhorrent to her and she could not imagine how she was going to get through an evening in any kind of proximity with Dominique.

Below her window the garden lay, calm and tranquil in the glow of the sunset. Impossible to believe in the ugly scene that had spoiled its idyllic atmosphere so shortly before, Lissa thought.

She stood, her fingers restlessly drumming on the panes. Was it possible that Dominique's monstrous allegation was true? Certainly it would explain much of Raoul's equivocal attitude towards Françoise, but if so what a mass of ugliness and misery was uncovered. Lissa shivered, and folded her arms across her breasts.

It explained so much else too, including Raoul's remarks about the possible ruin of Paul's life if their affair were to continue. If he himself had known a marriage that had slipped so far from the ideal, then his concern for Paul was more understandable.

But he had still no right to make assumptions about her, Lissa argued to herself. She had to keep her anger against Raoul in ferment. It would be too dangerous to allow treacherous emotions like sympathy and regret well up in her feelings about him. And how could he behave as he did to Françoise, who was after all so completely innocent?

She remembered with a pang how she had spoken to Raoul only that morning, accusing him of failing to love Françoise as his own. Every word she had uttered must have been like a stab wound, she realised. No wonder he had been angry! It was only surprising that he had retained as much control as he had.

She turned away from the window with relief as Maggie came in.

'Great news!' her godmother said gaily. 'Anne-Marie is downstairs.'

'That's wonderful!' In spite of her inner disturbance, Lissa was genuinely delighted at the thought of seeing Anne-Marie again. 'When did she arrive?'

'About an hour ago, I believe. She's brought her flatmate with her—a nice child named Nicole, who's some kind of cousin, I believe.' Maggie sighed. 'If the fair Dominique would just take herself off home, it would be a very pleasant family party. But I don't think there's any hope of that. She's hanging on until she snares Monsieur le Comte.'

'Do you think he will marry her?' Lissa spoke carefully past a sudden constriction in her throat.

'I think it's possible,' Maggie gave Lissa a shrewd glance. 'She has a lot in her favour, you know, what with the two families being in the same line of business and having known each other for years. And no matter how she may treat the rest of us, she's always honey to Raoul, and men are such fools with a certain type of woman. They never look below the surface. And from a hint that Madame gave me the other day I think his first marriage was a pretty stormy affair. He may not want to get out of his emotional depth a second time, and may just settle for a good-looking hostess, who'll leave him in peace in return for a generous dress allowance.'

'How cold-blooded,' Lissa shuddered. She felt a sudden chill, and picked up her black crocheted shawl from the bed and placed it round her shoulders.

'That is not a description that I would have fitted to Monsieur Raoul. However, we shall see what we shall see,' Maggie said. 'Shall we go down?'

Nicole d'Aubray was a slender dark-haired girl with a Madonna-like face, and a quiet air which contrasted attractively with Anne-Marie's more lively personality. Lissa could imagine how well the two got on together in their Paris *apartement*, and thought with a pang of Jenny, safely and happily engaged to Roger and making plans for her wedding. How uncomplicated it had all been for them once, before the de Gue brothers had come on the scene, she thought ruefully.

To her surprise, she learned from Anne-Marie that Nicole's shyness concealed a talent for fabric design that had taken her almost to the top of the art department in Fontaine's Paris house. She was even more surprised when Anne-Marie casually revealed that Nicole had been responsible for the Bacchante design that she had seen on that unforgettable first night with Raoul in London.

'But it was absolutely beautiful!' she exclaimed, turning to Nicole, who flushed slightly and murmured something in disclaimer.

'She is too modest,' said Anne-Marie. 'That design has been a *succès fou*.'

'How in the world do you get your ideas?' Lissa asked with genuine interest.

Nicole shrugged, flushing a little. 'I forget how that one came to me. I think it was just the coming of spring and all it means. Everyone hopes a little, I think, in springtime, and I wanted to create something that would convey those hopes and desires.'

'You must show Lissa some of your other designs,' Anne-Marie insisted. 'There is one that would suit her as if created for her.'

'Don't tell me,' Lissa said uncomfortably. 'Midsummer Night.'

Nicole's face showed her surprise. 'That's true. I

thought of it as I saw you. But how did you know?'

'I saw a sample once.' Lissa thought of the parcel hastily bundled to the back of her wardrobe and her face flamed, especially when she realised that Raoul de Gue, who was sitting on a nearby sofa with Dominique, could not have failed to overhear at least part of the conversation.

The length of dress fabric had never been mentioned between them, and it was impossible that it should be, Lissa thought. It revived too many memories that were best forgotten.

'I shall be working in the studio over the next few days on some special work that Raoul has commissioned from me, but I would be happy to show you some of our current fabrics,' said Nicole. There was an odd constraint in her manner, Lissa thought. Was it possible that Nicole did not like her? Surely not. There had been none of that instant antagonism that she had felt with Dominique, and yet ... Lissa could not put her finger on it, but there was something, some slight constraint that was more than just normal shyness. She was a little disappointed that her own immediate liking had not been fully returned.

'Thank you,' she said, taking up what she felt had been a slightly reluctant invitation with enthusiasm. 'I should love to see them. But you mentioned a studio. Where is that?'

Anne-Marie gasped. 'You didn't know? Has Paul never mentioned ... but of course not. He takes so little interest in the business these days. But yes, *ma chère*, we have a studio here in the Chateau. It was set up in Grandpère's day, because he believed a few days in the quiet of the country could often produce—what is that expression—"a fresh slant" for a designer. Besides, he had talent himself, and he and Madame Grand'mère often used to sketch out ideas up there

138

together which the art department would then later develop. It was a very good arrangement, although they did not always agree on what was good design.' She laughed. 'Grandpère preferred the abstract look, but Madame Grand'mère loved flowers and leaves, anything that was simple and fresh like her beloved garden. She said all her best ideas started there.'

'I would love to meet her,' Lissa said, impulsively.

'*Eh bien*,' Anne-Marie waved her hands vaguely. 'So you will when your engagement to Paul is made public. I expect he will take you down to Antibes to visit her. Her health is not so good for travelling these days.'

Lissa felt all the strain of her old embarrassment returning. 'No doubt,' she murmured, and turned back to Nicole only to intercept a look of real pain in the dark eyes before the long lashes were swiftly lowered, and Nicole retreated once more behind her barrier of reserve.

Lissa felt as if a light had just been switched on in a totally darkened room. 'Of course!' she told herself in bewilderment. 'She's in love with Paul. She must be. That's why she's so quiet with me. I must be a torment to her.'

For a moment she toyed with the idea of telling Nicole the truth as soon as they were alone together, but reluctantly she abandoned the idea. It was up to Paul to extricate them both, she decided, and it would be wrong to interfere when she had not the slightest idea what his feelings for Nicole were, if any.

Certainly Paul was emerging in a very different light from the gay and charming companion of their London days. It was perhaps a good thing she had not allowed her feelings to become too deeply involved, otherwise she might now find herself in the unenviable position of both Nicole and Dominique, both of whom seemed to have reason to think they had a prior claim on his affections.

'Nicole's too good for him,' Lissa decided. 'But if she wants him, she's the quietly determined type who could probably take him and make something out of him.'

She was reminded suddenly of something that Jenny had once said—that being in love made one more perceptive to other people's emotional problems. It seemed to be true as far as she was concerned, she thought wryly, and her heart twisted painfully at the thought of all she would be leaving behind her.

Anne-Marie was speaking again. 'Nicole has not been very well lately—a *petite malade*—so Raoul has decreed a rest with us here for a week or two.'

'He is always so considerate,' Nicole said with a note of real affection.

'Raoul always cherishes what he values most,' Anne-Marie laughed.

Lissa felt suddenly bleak. Other girls received his thoughtful consideration. All she had to remember was the bruising pressure of his mouth and hands. He could not have demonstrated his contempt for her more plainly, she thought drearily.

At that moment, Dominique joined the group. She was immaculately dressed as usual in a striking shade of deep red and she smelt extravagantly of some deep musky scent.

'*Bon soir*, Nicole,' she said, after coolly acknowledging the presence of Lissa and Anne-Marie. '*Quelle surprise*! I did not expect you would be visiting here—at this time particularly.'

There was a silence, and Lissa felt her face flaming. It was obvious to what Dominique was referring—her supposed engagement to Paul, and it was also obvious that it was a deliberate attempt to hurt the other girl.

It took only one look at Nicole's face, paler than ever, and with a curiously stricken look, to know that her suspicions about Nicole's feelings for Paul were correct.

How unnecessary of Dominique, and how typical, she thought, but Nicole was speaking.

'I am always happy to be at St Denis,' she said with gentle dignity. 'It has always been like a second home to me.'

'Good for you,' Lissa silently applauded, but Dominique had not finished yet.

'But everyone, *hélas,* must leave home eventually,' she said smoothly, adjusting the set of her dress over her curved hips. 'No one would ever wish to outstay their welcome.'

Her meaning was unmistakable. There would be no place for Nicole at the Chateau, once there was a new mistress at the Chateau, whether it was Raoul or Paul who married first. Lissa was in no doubt that Dominique was fully aware that Nicole was still in love with Paul, and that she was simply enjoying a malicious triumph over a former rival.

Her thoughts were made no happier by the arrival of Paul, carrying a fringed pastel stole over his arm, which he brought to Nicole.

'Your wrap, *chérie.* We must take care of you and make sure there are no more chills.'

Nicole thanked him, but her air of constraint was even more pronounced, and Lissa saw Anne-Marie give her a troubled look.

Feeling as if she could bear the tangle she was in no longer, now that it was obvious that it was causing hurt to someone else, Lissa murmured a swift excuse and moved swiftly across the room to the door. She ran across the hallway and had reached the stairs when an imperative 'Mademoiselle!' from behind her halted her in her tracks.

Raoul de Gue came at a leisurely pace across the hall and stood looking up at her.

'This is not the first time I have seen you flying for sanctuary while you have been under my roof,' he said, his slanting black brows raised questioningly. 'May I know what has disturbed you on this occasion?'

'I am not in the least disturbed.' Lissa faced him with a calmness she did not in the least feel.

'You are a liar,' he returned equally calmly. 'But as you are a guest in my house, I will have to accept what you say, I suppose, as a polite fiction and wait until you feel prepared to tell me the real truth in your own good time.'

Lissa lifted her chin.

'Being your guest has not protected me from your bullying in the past, *monsieur*.'

He leaned one arm on the balustrade and stared at her, drawing deeply on his cigarette.

'You consider me a bully,' he said meditatively. 'It is the first time I have been told that by a woman.'

'Indeed?' Lissa raised her eyebrows. 'Obviously your other women have been too cowed by your autocratic manner ever to venture an opinion.'

'My other women?' He blew a smoke ring reflectively. 'By implication, *ma belle*, that would seem to include you among them. As yet, you are not, you know. A few kisses do not make up the ultimate submission, as I thought you would have known only too well. Although I must admit your delicious response the other day brought us nearer to that moment of delight than I would ordinarily have hoped in so short a time.'

Lissa could have stamped with vexation, but she decided it would be wiser to ignore the last part of what he had said.

'You are deliberately twisting my words,' she accused him.

'Sparks suit those eyes far better than the tears I suspect I saw when I followed you just now,' he returned.

'You enjoy goading me.'

'It is a mutual pleasure, surely.' He paused, eyeing her, then held out his hand. 'Come down. Come back to the salon. Is it something that Dominique has said to you that has caused you distress? She will not upset you for much longer, after all.' Lissa stared at him, not comprehending, then he went on smoothly, 'Madame Desmond will soon have finished here, she assures me, and you will both be returning to London in a matter of days, I understand.'

She looked at him steadily, despising herself for the sudden hope that she prayed he had not seen revealed in her face. She still had some remnants of pride left.

'You will have to excuse me for this evening, *monsieur*. I have a slight headache. I think I have not yet quite recovered from my riding accident. I shall spend the evening in my room. And while I think of it, I must thank you for not revealing the truth of my stupid behaviour to Madame la Comtesse and my godmother. It was—good of you.'

'Your servant, *mademoiselle*. I know the effort it must have cost you to speak those words,' he said blandly. 'To have to acknowledge that I have some chivalrous impulses must have cost you dear.'

'Particularly when I know that any chivalry you display towards me is only a veneer,' she slammed back at him.

'Oh, I wouldn't say that.' He swung himself lightly on to the step beside her. 'I feel most chivalrous at this moment. Shall I carry you to your room, if you feel unwell? I have a collection of invalids under my roof at the moment, it seems. Nicole is also unwell, as you may have noticed, but she is mainly suffering from unrequited love, *pauvre petite*. The same cannot be said for you, can it, *ma belle*?' He reached out and gripped her wrist. His dark eyes looked down into hers with a penetration that sent her senses shaking. The scent of his cigarette, the warm clean smell of him filled her nostrils, and she felt faint with longing.

'Let me go,' she said, fighting for her control.

'And see you collapse at my feet? You are trembling like a leaf. An attentive host could not abandon you at such a moment.' He smiled. 'Shall I carry you to bed—*mademoiselle*?' His hand drew her closer. His dark face filled her vision. His mouth was barely inches from her own. 'Shall I carry you?' he repeated.

'*Nom de Dieu*, what is this?' Paul's voice, sharp with alarm and something like resentment, spoke from the hall below, and Lissa knew a flood of relief and yet at the same time her awakened senses trembled in frustration.

Raoul was the first to move. 'Your fiancée is feeling faint. She is still suffering some ill effects from her fall. I offered to help her to her room when she became dizzy.'

Paul joined them. 'Lissa,' his eyes were anxious, 'are you all right?'

'I think I would like to lie down.' Lissa looked at him, summoning every scrap of appeal of which she was capable.

'Of course, *chérie*.' To her chagrin, Paul leaned forward and brushed her lips with his own. Impossible to draw away under Raoul's mocking gaze. Cold with misery, she submitted, and as Paul put a protective arm around her and began to lead her upstairs, she heard the click of the salon door closing, and knew they were alone.

Once in her bedroom, an attempt to discover from

Paul what his feelings had been for Nicole drew unusually evasive answers, to Lissa's annoyance.

'You know how these things are, *chérie*,' he said airily, toying with the brushes and scent sprays on her dressing table.

'I'm certainly beginning to,' Lissa returned, angrily. 'And what was I, precisely? Just another of those things?'

'But no. How can you think of such a thing? I love you, my beautiful Lissa. To you I offered my heart and my whole life.'

'I'm not really in the market for shop-soiled goods,' Lissa snapped, allowing her temper to betray her into a deliberately cruel remark. But she relented when she saw him wince. It was not altogether Paul's fault that he had been born with more of the world's goods and attractions than most other men. And he was not completely spoiled. He had begun, as she knew from their early morning rides together, to start to take an interest in his new job of estate management, and only made superficial references of regret about his former playboy existence in Paris and London.

'Paul,' she said more gently, 'I think it's time we told everyone the truth.'

'What do you mean?' He stared at her.

'I mean that this charade has gone on long enough, and you must know it by now.'

'But we agreed...'

'Yes,' Lissa said desperately, 'I know that. But I don't think it's necessary any longer. For one thing, I think your mother has a strong suspicion that there is nothing between us, so she won't be upset. And surely you've realised that Dominique isn't interested in you any more.'

Paul lit himself a cigarette with a marked snap of his lighter, and Lissa realised she had not been very

145

tactful. Paul might regard marriage with Dominique as a fate worse than death, but that did not mean she could merely lose interest in him at will.

He likes to be the centre of attention still, she thought. He has to prove to himself that he is irresistible to women at all times. His wife, whoever she is, will need to be very understanding—more so than I could ever have been.

'Well, I think it would be madness to give up now,' Paul said stubbornly. 'Just when Raoul is convinced.'

'And that's another thing,' Lissa faced him with a flash of anger. 'Was there any need for these touching displays of affection over the past couple of days, and particularly on the stairs just now? That was not part of the bargain, let me remind you.'

He laughed easily. '*Eh bien*, it got rid of Raoul, didn't it, which was what you wanted—or was it?' He looked at her quizzically. 'You've changed, Lissa. You're not the girl I knew in London. Where did she go, I wonder?—And where did she give her heart, if not to me?'

'I don't think either of us has really changed, Paul,' Lissa told him. 'I think this time together has done one useful thing at least. It has shown us that we don't belong together. That was not perhaps what was originally intended, but...'

'No,' he looked moodily at the glowing butt of his cigarette, then crushed it into a porcelain ash tray. 'Oh, *diable*, Lissa—it was all a game, getting the better of Raoul at first, wasn't it? But now it has gone sour, hasn't it—for both of us?'

Lissa bent her head. 'Yes,' she agreed tonelessly.

'Poor Lissa!' he touched her hair lightly for a moment. 'But it won't be for much longer. You have my word.'

She smiled at him a little wanly. Probably they had

never cared so little about each other, and yet momentarily they were closer than they had been since their days in London.

It was a relief over the next few days to be shut up in the library with Maggie, who was well into her stride with the book, with pages of manuscript for transcription each morning and dictation every afternoon.

The weather had changed too, and a chilly wind blew scurries of rain against the windows, and made them glad of the log fire which was kindled daily in the hearth for them.

Often as she typed, while Maggie paced the room behind her, reading pages of script and sometimes murmuring approvingly, and at others crumpling them up and hurling them into the fire with strange oaths, Lissa thought about the garden, and what the wet weather would be doing to the weeds she had so nearly got under control.

Silly to care so much, when she would be leaving so soon, and the garden behind its high walls would revert to its old half-wild state again. Unless Dominique ... but no, that was too ludicrous even to contemplate. She would be one mistress of the Chateau who would not go to the garden to think over the little problems of day-to-day life as a wife and mother, or dream her dreams in its tranquillity.

Who would appreciate the roses, now at their best, when next year came. Would anyone have carried out the vital pruning, or trained the climbing rose back on to the piece of mended trellis? Would the lawns Lissa had clipped with such care become overgrown and wild again?

If the garden were hers to plan, she would buy more roses, she thought dreamily. Some had run too far to briar and should be discarded, and she would bring in some of the old-fashioned scented varieties as well as

147

the exotically coloured modern hybrids to add contrast and flair.

She sighed, and her fingers remained motionless on the typewriter keys until she became aware of Maggie's surprised gaze and returned to the task in hand with more speed than accuracy, finding herself with a spoiled sheet to re-type.

One day, while they were working, Maggie said casually, 'I think we can start making arrangements to go home at the end of next week. I've just about finished all I need here.'

'So soon?' Lissa began, and Maggie gave her a sharp look.

'I thought it couldn't be soon enough for you,' she said.

Well, that was true, Lissa thought, or it had been at least. The last thing she wanted, certainly, was to be here to see Dominique's triumph at last.

'At least the weather is clearing up,' she remarked with apparent lightness, looking out of the window. 'I must get some work done in the garden before we leave.'

Maggie gave her a look which combined shrewdness with sympathy.

'Not leaving too many attachments, I hope, ducky? —and I don't mean merely a rambling rose or two.'

'No.' Lissa straightened her back and spoke vehemently. 'I'll leave without a backward glance.'

'Hmm,' Maggie said sceptically. 'Now let's turn back for a moment to the ending of chapter six. I'm not entirely convinced about the Comte's reaction there.'

She waited while Lissa riffled through the pages of script, then added casually, 'How history does tend to repeat itself!'

But when Lissa glanced at her, her face was bland.

and there was not even the trace of a twinkle in her eye.

Lissa had not forgotten her silent pledge to herself regarding Françoise and she made a point of seeking the little girl out later that day before she went to the garden.

The roses, they found, were looking their best after the rain, and when Françoise suggested picking a bunch for her father's desk in the library, Lissa agreed with alacrity. It would be a useful overture in her self-appointed campaign to reconcile Raoul with his daughter and convince him that the story he had been told was a vicious lie.

For in spite of Dominique's positive and spiteful assertion, she was convinced that Françoise was Raoul's child and that his wife, for some reason best known to herself, had deliberately lied. Their marriage must have been in a disastrous state for her to have even contemplated saying such a thing, Lissa thought sorrowfully.

But Françoise was so like him. They had the same high-bridged nose, their chins bore the same determined cleft, and they shared that arrogant turn of the head. How could Raoul not see it? How could he not see Françoise reproduced a dozen times in the portraits and miniatures in the galleries? Shock and horror, and the knowledge that his wife had betrayed him with other men, must have blinded him to the truth, she thought.

Again an inward voice argued that it was none of her business and that she was facing yet another metaphorical slap in the face from the Comte if she interfered again. Yet her sense of what was right and just would not allow her simply to abandon the situation. Besides, she had grown to love Françoise.

After all the lies and deception to which she had been an unwilling party since her arrival at the Chateau, she could at least establish the truth on one point, she told herself.

She gave Françoise the secateurs and supervised closely as the child operated them, picking the choicest blooms that would open to their full glory once they were in the house.

They had just finished and Françoise was gloating openly over her handiwork, when voices were heard and to Lissa's surprise Paul entered the garden accompanied by Nicole. She was less pleased to see Dominique bringing up the rear, and with an oddly protective feeling she drew Françoise towards her and told her to run back to the house and ask Madame Barrat for a bowl in which to arrange the roses.

'Put them in the library and we'll do them presently,' she urged, and the little girl ran off obediently.

Nicole was looking round with shining eyes. 'Oh, but it is so beautiful! Mademoiselle Fairfax must have—what is the English phrase?—green fingers. It was a wilderness, and now it is a haven of loveliness.'

'It should be,' Paul said good-humouredly. 'The amount of time she has spent here has been *incroyable*. Whenever Madame Desmond has no need of her, she cannot be found and—*voilà!*'

'Is this how the English make love, perhaps?' Dominique, of course. 'Grubbing in the earth at a man's feet! How odd, is it not, Nicole? I prefer, me, to have the man at my feet, don't you?'

Nicole flushed unhappily, and Lissa gave her a compassionate look. She began to put the secateurs and other tools she had been using back into the basket, as Dominique went on.

'It's so warm and sheltered here, it's wasted as a garden. It would make a marvellous site for a swimming pool. Think of it, Paul—all paved with tables and loungers round it, and an oval pool in the centre simply inviting one to dive in, especially on a day like this. Sheer heaven!'

'I think,' said Paul, 'that while Madame Grand'mère is alive it will remain a garden. I also think this would be Raoul's view.

Dominique gave him a limpid look. '*Peut-être*,' she murmured. 'But Raoul can always be persuaded to change his mind, *enfin*.'

She turned to Lissa. 'I should not waste so much time on your knees, *mademoiselle*. There will be no one to appreciate your efforts when you return to London.'

Lissa bit her lip. Any number of retorts occurred to her, but how could she use any of them without hurting Nicole even further and causing a scene, which she herself wished to avoid at this juncture? Instead she smiled.

'I've had enough of the sun today, Mademoiselle Nicole. Shall we go back to the house?'

Nicole agreed at once, and insisted on helping to carry some of the tools back to the stable, where Pierre greeted them with his usual air of humouring lunatics.

'Have you done any work since you have been here?' Lissa asked, as she and Nicole left the stable and walked back towards the kitchen area.

'A little.' Nicole hesitated. 'You said you would like to see the studio. Would it be convenient now, perhaps?'

'Is it near?' Lissa asked, looking round doubtfully.

'Very near,' Nicole smiled. 'Come, this way.' And she led the way to a door in the corner of the stable buildings which looked considerably newer and with fresher paintwork, Lissa noticed, than the surrounding woodwork.

Inside a modern open plan staircase led upwards into what must have been a big loft. Now, it was a perfect studio, with a new wood-block floor and huge windows let into the roof and two walls of the room. There were easels and boxes of pastels and colours lying around, and even some bolts of fabrics heaped on trestle tables in a corner. Nicole picked up some large folders and untied the strings that held them.

'We are planning our autumn collection now, you understand. I call this one Autumn Sigh.' She passed Lissa a sheet glowing with russet and grey tones, with an elusive thread of gold running through the mistiness of the general effect. Lissa was enthralled, as she looked through the folder, exclaiming with delight when one particular beauty caught her eye.

'I think we have similar tastes, you and I, *mademoiselle*,' Nicole said, then paused and bit her lip, as she realised what she had said.

Lissa felt dreadful. 'Perhaps not in everything, *mademoiselle*,' she said gently. 'And I wish we could drop this formality. I would like you to call me Lissa.'

'*Certainement*.' Nicole looked at her with a certain wistfulness. 'I would like us to be friends.'

Lissa roamed round the room, looking at half-finished sketches, and samples of colours on some of the easels. Eventually in one corner she came on a large drawing board, with a covering sheet turned towards the wall.

'What's this? The *pièce de résistance*?' she laughed, turning it over, before Nicole's 'Ah, no, Lissa—that is most private,' could prevent her.

She could understand immediately why it was private. It was a design that could only have been meant for a wedding dress. The underlying shade was a rich ivory, but traced on it was a delicate design in silver translucence that could only have been roses. It was one of the most perfect and romantic designs for a wedding gown that Lissa had ever seen, and she stared at it transfixed.

'I'm sorry if I've intruded,' she said at last, as Nicole came across and replaced the covering sheet and the board to its former position.

'It was my own fault. I should have warned you. Some of our designs are most exclusive and can be seen by no one. And when it is for the *patron* himself at his own order . . .' Nicole smiled and shrugged apologetically. 'He gave most strict instructions that it should be seen by no one.'

'It is for the Comte himself?' Lissa felt a cold sick feeling in the pit of her stomach.

'A very special order—hush-hush, as you say—and very rushed too. I think he has decided to give St Denis a Comtesse again at last. He told me exactly what he wanted before he brought me down here. It is to be called Jour des Noces—Wedding Day.'

Lissa felt she wanted to escape, to run away from the sunny studio, and even from Nicole, sublimely unconscious of Lissa's utter despair. So arrangements had even proceeded that far, she thought.

'It will be very becoming,' she commented, deliberately torturing herself by thinking of Dominique in the full glory of the gown, with the veil and train and the de Gue necklace much in evidence.

'It was a privilege to be asked to design it. I think Raoul wanted the secret kept in the family.' Nicole's voice took on that slight note of constraint again. 'I suppose, therefore, there is no harm in your knowing about it.'

Lissa decided the time had come to tell the truth at last. She could bear the look in Nicole's eyes no longer.

'Nicole,' she said gently, 'I'm not engaged to Paul—I never have been. It has all been a trick that he asked me to play on Raoul for reasons I would rather not go into. He may tell you himself one day, and I hope he does. I wanted you to know because I know you have been unhappy, and that it was partly my fault and because—well, I know exactly how you feel. That's all.'

Impulsively, she bent forward and kissed the other girl on the cheek, then she turned and ran to the door, down the stairs and back into the stable yard, drawing in deep gulping breaths of fresh air.

She heard Mistral, who knew her step by now, whinny, and forcing herself to calmness walked over to the loosebox where the big bay was watching for her coming, his liquid eyes alive with hope for titbits.

Lissa reached up and put her arms round his glossy neck, burying her face in his coat, oblivious to anyone who might be watching.

'Oh, Mistral,' she whispered brokenly, 'what am I going to do? I love him so!'

# CHAPTER NINE

SHE had recovered her composure by the time she reached the library where Françoise was eagerly waiting for her with an elegant silver rose bowl, and even some crumpled chicken wire to use as a base that Madame Barrat had produced from somewhere.

As they worked companionably, Lissa showed Françoise how to remove the worst of the thorns, so that their fingers would not become lacerated as they arranged the flowers.

'Have you been to the village lately?' Lissa asked with apparent casualness as they experimented with different groupings of blossoms.

Françoise shook her head. 'It has been too wet for us to go walking. Besides, I don't...' She did not finish the sentence, hanging her head.

'You don't like going there because the other children are not very friendly,' Lissa supplied intuitively. 'Why is that, *petite*? What happened? Have you never played with them. They seemed to know you.'

Françoise nodded vigorously. 'When Mademoiselle Bertrand was my *gouvernante* I often used to play down by the river with the others. I liked them and we had many happy games. I was even learning to swim in the big pool by the bridge where it is safe. But then Mademoiselle Bertrand's mother became ill and she had to go away to look after her, and then Mademoiselle Firaud came. She said I was not to play with the children from St Denis because I was the daughter of the Chateau and must behave as such—according to my station in life, she said. She would not even let me speak to Yvonne or Michelle or anyone to explain, and now they call me *"petite poseuse"* and make fun of me.'

Poor kid, Lissa thought compassionately. What an existence! No young people at the Chateau to play with, and now cut off from the only playmates she had ever known through some outworn snobbery. No wonder the village children had been offended by her sudden defection, and Françoise was lucky if 'little snob' was the only accusation that had come her way. Her blood boiled inwardly and her fingers itched to take hold of Mademoiselle Firaud and shake her.

'Who recommended Mademoiselle Firaud to be your *gouvernante?*' she asked, again trying to sound casual.

*'Je crois que c'était* Dominique. Mademoiselle had been employed by a family that Dominique's parents knew, but the children of the family went away to school, and she came here. I wish she hadn't,' Françoise added in a sudden burst of candour. 'It is so dull with her, and I do not think she likes me greatly.'

Lissa decided it would be wiser to disregard this part of Françoise's remarks.

'But would you like to play with the village children again? You don't feel that you are different or—better in some way than they are?'

*'Eh bien, non!'* Françoise stared at her in frank disbelief. 'Why Angèle Ducros can skip for hours and Monique can swim across the pool and back. I was only learning to do these things,' she added forlornly. 'But I think they will not want me back with them now.'

'Oh, I wouldn't say that,' Lissa said cheerfully. 'It may take some time, and you will need quite a bit of courage, but I think, if you want them enough, they will accept you back as one of them again.'

Françoise threw her arms round Lissa's neck and

assured her fervently that was what she did want, and Lissa made a mental note to take the first step towards Françoise's re-integration process with her former friends as soon as possible. She would even take the child swimming herself in the big pool at first, and when she had gone back to London, Anne-Marie, who would undoubtedly be scandalised and angry if she knew the truth, could carry on the good work.

But at the same time she was unhappily aware that when Dominique married Raoul, Mademoiselle Firaud would probably become a permanent part of the ménage, and her snobbish values would have plenty of time and opportunity to take root in a child as young and impressionable as Françoise. It would probably also put a stop towards any hope of the child being sent to school eventually, which Lissa thought would do her the world of good.

Suddenly she was aware that they were no longer alone, and swung round to see Raoul de Gue leaning in the doorway watching them. He wore a dark lounge suit, with a dazzling white shirt and a tie so elegant it could have been one of Fontaine's own designs, and even though he looked slightly forbidding in his formal clothes, he was still the most devastatingly attractive man Lissa had ever seen, and she had to restrain an entirely feminine impulse to lift her hands and tidy back some stray fronds of hair.

'All the work in Madame Grand'mère's garden has not been in vain, I see,' he commented, but there was no hint of either pleasure or censure in his voice.

'I hoped you wouldn't mind. Françoise wanted so much to pick some roses for your desk. I thought it would be an improvement. It always seems so bare.'

There she went again, interfering, she thought miserably. 'Now he'll tell me that it's a working desk with no room for frivolities like flowers.'

But to her surprise he smiled slightly. 'You think I should have a daily rose in a crystal vase and family photographs in silver frames, like some American tycoon?' he inquired with an upward tilt of his dark brows.

'No, of course not. But flowers do make a room more—homely,' Lissa said a little lamely.

'Unfortunately I have not tended to regard this house as my home for some years,' Raoul returned, and there was a note of bitterness in his voice which struck an echoing pang with Lissa.

She turned to Françoise who was deliberating between a pink rosebud and a crimson rose already half open, and said quickly, 'I think some of that lovely fern would finish the bowl off really well. You know— the one I showed you the last time we were in the garden. Run and get some quickly and we'll experiment.'

Françoise obeyed eagerly, letting herself out of the French windows which gave on to a neat gravelled walk and a lawn beyond.

'You have a way with children,' Raoul remarked. 'I have never seen her so animated.'

Lissa looked at him steadily. 'The question is do you see her at all?'

'We have already had this conversation, *mademoiselle*, and I believe I made it clear to you that you are on dangerous ground, I am not prepared to discuss the child with you.'

'I am not subject to your edicts, *monsieur*.' Lissa spoke formally, but anger was fighting with love and compassion for him in her emotions. She was determined to remain calm this time and say what she knew must be said.

'Please, please, Raoul—listen to me.' She faltered a little as she realised she had used his name for the first time since she had come to the Chateau, then went on quickly, 'I won't take up much of your time, I promise. But I can't leave here next week without telling you first what I believe—what I *know* is the truth.'

'Are you capable of the truth? Is any woman?' The bite in his voice chilled her. 'Very well.' Reluctantly he drew a silver case from his pocket, extracted a cigarette and lit it. 'Say what you must, but do not blame anyone but yourself if you go too far. I have taken about as much as I can stand from you—in every way.'

It was an unpromising start, and Lissa clenched her trembling hands into fists to give her courage for a moment. Then, forcing calmness, she turned back to the remaining roses and began to slot them skilfully into the remaining spaces in her arrangement.

'I have been told a story about Françoise's birth,' she said. 'I think you have been told the same thing. But you believe it—and I don't. I can't. No one who has ever seen you together with Françoise could believe such a tissue of lies. Whatever you were told, and by whom, Raoul—Françoise is your daughter, your own flesh and blood. All you have to do is look in a mirror, and you will see yourself reflected in her. She's the image of you—looks, mannerisms—oh, everything!'

She faltered to a halt, her eyes blurred with tears. The man by the door had not stirred, and his face still wore its forbidding expression.

Lissa reached out blindly for a crimson rose and cried out as a large thorn still left on the stem ran deep into her hand. A drop of blood, no less crimson, welled up and ran down to her wrist as she fished awkwardly in the pocket of her jeans for a handkerchief or a tissue.

'You are hurt?' Raoul de Gue was at her side, but there was still no softening in his face.

'It's nothing. A mere prick.'

'Nonsense. You are bleeding.' He took the hand she was trying to hide behind her back and frowned as he examined the injury. 'There's a piece of the thorn left in the wound. It must come out before we put a dressing on it, or it may become poisoned,' he said.

Before she could stop him, he had bent his head and putting his mouth to her palm, had sucked out the thorn.

Lissa felt her body melting. The intimate touch of his mouth against the soft swell of the mound below her thumb destroyed her defences. Her plea for Françoise, her determination to tell him the truth about her relationship with Paul all disappeared under the frantic desire to feel his mouth again, only this time against her own.

'I hope I did not hurt you.' His tone was cool and courteous as he stepped back. He took a clean handkerchief from his breast pocket and improvised a neat bandage, while she stood mute, fighting for her self-control.

'Ask Madame Barrat later for a proper dressing. I think it is clean, but we cannot be too careful,' he said.

'Nothing I have said to you has made the slightest difference, has it?' Lissa asked quietly.

'As you seem to know so much of my personal story, you may as well hear the rest,' he said. 'Sit down.'

'I prefer to stand.'

'And I prefer you to sit. *Assieds-toi.*' He pressed her down into a chair, his hard fingers compressing her shoulder.

'It's not a pleasant story, but you have already heard what is probably the worst of it. I met Victoire, my late wife, in Paris. She was a model and had done some work for Fontaine. That was how we met, *naturelle-ment*. She was the most beautiful thing I had ever seen, and I wanted her. I had other women—in my position, with my wealth, it was no problem and never had been. But Victoire was different. She wanted a name—respectability and above all money. I fitted her bill most admirably. Consequently it was made clear to me that without the sacred bonds of matrimony, her lovely body was to be denied me. I did not know her motives then. I suppose in some besotted way I put it down to virginal reluctance and respected her for it. *Dieu, quel idiot!*'

He paused and drew deeply on his cigarette. 'I didn't know of course that the reason it was never convenient for me to call at her *apartement* without a prior appointment was because she was entertaining other—admirers. She did not wish to jeopardise them or her relationship with me. She was really very clever about it.'

He walked over to the window and stood gazing out. 'Eventually, we married,' he said. 'We came here to live. It was a disaster. She hated everything to do with the life. All she cared about was clothes and admirers. Here, she had nowhere to show off her creations, and no admirers, except for Paul who was too callow then, even for her tastes. So she began making trips to Paris again—to look up old friends, as she put it.'

Lissa found her voice. 'But Françoise?'

'An accident,' he said heavily. 'That's what she said at first, blaming it on one of the few occasions that we had shared a bed. She had a difficult pregnancy and a hard labour. The doctors feared for her life, but she lived, and I, knowing I had put her through this ordeal, knelt by her bed, thanking her for this gift she had given me—for this tiny, precious Françoise who had fought so tenaciously for her life. And then she laughed. We were alone, of course, for this moment of tender reunion. She laughed—weak as she was. She was obliged for my gratitude, she said, but she could

161

not guarantee it was due from me. And she named four other men who could—any of them—have been Françoise's father.'

'Oh, God,' Lissa said faintly. 'Don't tell me any more. It's not right. It's too private—too intimate.'

'You asked for it. You would know. And you would have had to know one day anyway. Now you can listen. For the next year or so we lived together on the surface only. Divorce was unthinkable, but we agreed we would not live as man and wife again.

'Every time I saw the child I was torn in two. I wanted to love her as my own, yet at the same time I was tormented by these doubts. Each time we quarrelled, it was Victoire's final weapon. Her visits to Paris became more frequent, and she took no interest in the child, the business of this house. We engaged a good nurse who looked after Françoise, and Victoire left the baby here with her almost permanently.

'Even when Françoise became ill, Victoire wasn't even slightly troubled. I told her the child was sick and needed her and she laughed in my face.' He stubbed the cigarette out savagely in an onyx ash tray.

'She was leaving me, she said. Going to a man with more money—a Greek shipping magnate, I think he was—her passport to the Jet Set. I had just been a stepping stone up the social scale for her.'

He looked at Lissa, his face twisted with the kind of torment she had never seen possess anyone in her life. Instinctively she wanted to run to him, to draw his face down to hers for her kisses, to smooth away the lines of strain with her caresses and woo him with her body until he lost sight of all past pain and sorrow in the sweet oblivion of love. But she did not dare, terrified of a rebuff, still hampered by the knowledge that she was still deceiving him herself. So she sat where she was, her fingers endlessly twisting the ends of the handkerchief he had bandaged round her hand.

'The rest,' he said, 'your kind informant has no doubt already told you—that she left Françoise delirious and calling for her, to drive to Paris to meet her lover, and was killed trying to beat an express train on a crossing.'

'Oh, no!' Lissa leaned forward, her face urgent. 'I never heard that. I heard that she was hurrying to be with the child when an accident happened—with a lorry. Something like that.'

'That was the story that was put around,' he admitted, digging his hands savagely into his pockets. 'The servants, especially Thérèse, are loyal, praise to *le bon Dieu*. They knew or guessed the situation, but no one ever said anything—until now.' He eyed Lissa. 'I should be interested to know who has chosen to spread this venom to you.'

Lissa lifted her chin, in spite of the fact that her eyes were full of tears and she wanted nothing so much as complete solitude in which to break her heart in peace for this lonely child and equally lonely man driven apart by the evil spite of a discontented woman. Probably, Lissa thought, a choking feeling in her throat, it was her revenge on Raoul both for her pregnancy and the pain she had suffered in the birth itself.

'I am waiting for an answer, *mademoiselle*.'

'I have no intention of telling you, *monsieur*. If it is any consolation to you, I was told for a deliberate purpose and not as mere idle gossip. I was intended to be hurt by the news.'

'And were you?' His eyes were suddenly intent, but she did not see as she gazed down at her bandaged hand.

'Naturally. I am very fond of Françoise, as you have noticed.'

'Ah,' he said quietly, and there was a long pause.

Then he murmured half to himself, 'I see.' and walked towards her.

Lissa stiffened, but he made no attempt to touch her, but threw himself into the big leather swivel chair on the opposite side of the desk, putting out his hand to touch the petals of the roses.

'There were always roses on this desk when Madame Grand'mère lived here,' he remarked almost idly, as if the previous conversation had never taken place. 'And when there were no roses, always there was a bowl of other flowers or leaves for Grandpère to look at from her dreaming garden.' He traced the delicate moulding of one gold-tipped pink beauty with his finger. 'It was Victoire who drove Madame Grand'mère away to Antibes. She said it was the climate, but we all knew differently. Victoire had the power of hurting—like the thorn you discovered in that rose, *ma belle*. She seemed almost to enjoy it.'

And Dominique is just such another, Lissa thought achingly. She remembered a discussion her parents had once had about a neighbour who had married for the second time a wife as shrewish and sharp-tongued as his first had been. 'A glutton for punishment,' her father had called him, and the story had always made her smile. But not now. Now it was too personal, too real. She thought of Raoul's taut, drawn face and Françoise's shy overtures of friendship which might soon be quenched for ever by an uncaring, unloving stepmother. Oh, Raoul, not you! she thought, fighting the tight feeling in her throat.

'I have been meaning to thank you for all you have done in the walled garden for some time. Madame Grand'mère would be delighted if she could see it.' Raoul broke into her thoughts, his voice calm and courteous again, and Lissa forced herself to respond in the same way.

164

'It's nothing. I love gardening, and was glad to be out in the open air so much.' Her voice sounded mechanical and she was glad to have an innocuous subject to talk about at last. 'It's a pity that it will not remain a garden for much longer,' she added unguardedly, and could have bitten out her tongue.

Raoul, who was lighting another cigarette, looked up in surprise.

'What does that mean?'

Lissa twisted her hands unhappily in her lap. 'I believe there is a plan to turn it into a swimming pool.'

'Ah, yes,' he spoke meditatively. 'I believe Dominique has mentioned something of the sort to me on several occasions.'

'And what do you feel about it?' Lissa hardly dared ask the question.

He shrugged and tossed his lighter into the air, catching it deftly. 'I think that beautiful women tend to get their own way in the end, *ma belle*, don't you?'

Lissa hardly dared trust herself to answer and was saved by Françoise's reappearance with the fern.

Under Raoul de Gue's cynical gaze, Lissa felt all thumbs and Françoise was more enthusiastic than expert, but when the bowl was finished it looked most attractive, and a solemn debate followed as to where it would be seen to the best advantage.

Lissa noticed as they worked that Raoul's eyes were constantly on Françoise. He was not relaxed in his chair. His whole posture reminded her of some sleek wild cat rather like a panther poised to spring, and he was watching Françoise as if she was his prey. But she could not read the expression in his eyes. They were veiled by his heavy lids and enigmatic.

Lissa had never felt so wretched. She had been

wounded herself by what Raoul had told her. What could he have felt all these years? How could any woman have been so heartless? Now she could better understand his attitude towards herself, and with understanding came forgiveness.

His wife had been wanton, and he would not risk his younger brother, far more susceptible than himself, falling into the same trap. If she had been in his shoes, she would probably also have tried to put a stop to the affair, by fair means or foul, she was honest enough to admit. Yet she still could not find any explanation why he should think Paul could find happiness with Dominique. This was still a puzzle to her.

Now that Raoul had been so straight with her she felt the time was ripe for some mutual honesty, but with Françoise in the room it was impossible, and she could not invent another errand for the child on the spur of the moment.

As it was, the problem was solved when Maggie put her head round the door.

'There you are, ducky,' she said. 'I feel like a spot of dictation on the terrace this afternoon as it's so glorious, so bring your book, will you? I've had the most marvellous idea of how to get rid of that troublesome Armand!'

Lissa had to smile, and the tension in the room lifted perceptibly.

'You can finish the flowers, *ma petite*,' she told Françoise. 'Don't use too much fern, and then you can present it to Papa as your very own gift.'

She snatched up her notebook and followed Maggie through the hall and the small salon and out on to the terrace where some small tables and chairs and a number of comfortable loungers had been set out in the glorious sunshine.

Madame de Gue was seated at one, engaged with

some petit-point, but she merely waved and smiled and made no attempt to start any conversation as Maggie and Lissa got down to work.

Maggie had indeed been inspired, and after about ten minutes' solid dictation had elapsed, Lissa realised she would need another notebook. She excused herself quickly, leaving Maggie to sip iced Campari with soda, and ran back into the house to the library where she kept her spare stationery in a drawer in the desk.

The library door was ajar and made no noise as she pushed it open. Then she paused, not daring to move or make a sound.

Raoul de Gue was standing facing the large ornate mirror above the mantelpiece. He was holding Françoise in his arms and was gazing at them both in the mirror as if he was trying to memorise their every feature. As Lissa watched, transfixed, he reached round and pulled the child's face against his own almost roughly, kissing her cheeks and her eyes and stroking her hair, while Françoise wrapped her slender arms round his neck in a convulsive hug.

Lissa backed out unseen, her throat tight with tears, and her eyes blurred by an odd mist.

When she rejoined the others on the terrace a little later on, she found that her notebook would not be needed after all, as all work seemed to have stopped for the day. A newcomer had joined the group, all now gathered round one of the tables—a man with glasses and thinning hair whom she recognised almost immediately.

'Mr Prentiss!' she exclaimed.

Max Prentiss set down his glass and rose smiling. 'My dear Miss Fairfax, what a pleasure! I little thought when Raoul introduced us at the Bacchante showing weeks ago that I would meet you here—or as a future daughter-in-law of the house, if what I hear is true.'

Lissa groaned inwardly, and cast a helpless glance at Maggie who was studing the stem of her glass with more than usual interest. Madame de Gue, immaculate in cream linen, was also smiling benignly. Neither of them fortunately had read any significance into his reference to their earlier meeting.

She forced a smile. 'I think it's a slight exaggeration, Mr Prentiss. Nothing has been actually fixed yet.'

'But it will be. I know these de Gues. They get anything they set their minds on, believe me. That's why Fontaines are at the top of the tree.'

To Lissa's relief conversation became general at this point, much of it centring round the projected autumn collection of new fabrics.

'But where is Nicole?' Max Prentiss leaned back at his ease. 'She's the one I have to see. I heard she had not been too well, and that could spell disaster for us.'

'Nicole's troubles are more emotional than physical,' Madame de Gue said somewhat unexpectedly. 'But she spends each day in the studio, and she seems happier every day. As for her work, that goes well, as you must know by the special order that she has already produced at top speed.'

'You mean our secret?' Max Prentiss asked. 'Only Raoul seems to know anything about that. Perhaps there is some royal wedding in the offing that he knows of.'

Lissa was thankful when the subject was dropped at this juncture and she was amused to discover that Maggie and Max Prentiss had a number of mutual acquaintances in London, and had soon begun one of those exhaustive conversations involving relationships and anecdotes of no interest to anyone but themselves.

Somewhat at a loose end, she glanced around and saw the Comtesse beckoning to her. As she approached Madame produced the inevitable footstool from beneath her chair and Lissa sank on to it, feeling about as old as Françoise.

'So,' Madame said after a slight pause. 'Our little Nicole blooms in the sunshine like the roses you tend so lovingly in the garden. But you, *ma petite*, you have the suntan, but the face is much thinner. Your cheekbones and the hips stand out as they did not when you first arrived. You no longer have curves, but angles, and this is not good.'

'I'm all right, madame,' Lissa protested, but the Comtesse lifted a minatory hand.

'I like you Lissa, but I want you to tell me truth, which I think you have not always done. Are you in love with my son?'

Lissa was lost for an answer. 'Which son?' seemed her only reaction, but it would be impossible to say that without giving herself away completely.

At last she said quietly, 'Madame, I think you should know that Paul and I have decided that we should not be happy together after all, and that our engagement is at an end.'

'Paul?' Madame sounded astounded. 'But who mentioned Paul? It is Raoul of whom I speak. Do you love him?'

'Madame——' Lissa paused again helplessly. Her eyes fell to her injured hand still tightly swathed in his handkerchief and with a gesture that said more than words, she raised it for an instant to her cheek.

'I thought so,' Madame de Gue reached out and stroked the silky hair so close to her knee. 'I warn you, *petite*, you will not have an easy life. He has known one bitter disappointment. Only those of us who were here then can remember those dreadful times. So

169

Raoul has built a shell around his tenderest feelings. But the right woman could break through it, I think, and it is my belief, that you are the one.'

Lissa raised eyes full of wretchedness. 'I don't think he believes so, *madame*.'

'You did not see him, *ma mie*, on the day of your accident when he carried you into the house like one distraught. He was as pale as you. And while you were unconscious he refused to leave your side. He insisted he must wait in case you called for him.'

And she had called for him, Lissa thought numbly. Raoul's presence at her bedside had not been part of a confused dream after all. He had really been there.

Madame stroked her hair again. 'I wanted you to know, *petite*, that Paul has told me everything. I was angry at first, but I did not blame you. When one is young and has been angered as you were, one does things that in calmness you would not consider. I would still welcome you as a daughter to my family. It is time there was another English bride at St Denis.'

'But what about Dominique?' Lissa fiddled inconsequentially with one of the fringes on the footstool.

'What indeed! She is determined, that little one, and she wants one of my sons. If Raoul marries her, it will not be for love but as a business transaction, I think. She would make a suitable wife, *sans doute*, but with her he will never know the joy, pain and pleasure of sharing each moment as I knew with his father, and Raoul could know with you.'

Lissa, blushing furiously, murmured something incoherent in reply and was saved by Max Prentiss, who came across to her and held out his hand.

'Come and show me this English walled garden in the middle of France that I have heard so much about,' he invited. 'Anne-Marie has told me you have done wonders with it.'

Lissa was glad to make her escape. Her talk with Madame de Gue had shaken her deeply, and she knew she could only hurt them both by telling Madame that her hopes and dreams would never come true, and that she could never hope to find now the ecstasy she longed for in his arms.

# CHAPTER TEN

MAX PRENTISS turned out to be extremely knowledge-able about gardens and their upkeep, and he was full of praise at what Lissa had achieved in the compara-tively short time she had been at the Chateau.

'If only old Madame de Gue could see it, she would be delighted,' he said.

Lissa looked at him in some surprise. 'You knew her, then?'

'Oh, yes. It was not so many years ago that she left the Chateau for her present home, after all.' He laughed. 'She used to sit in that arbour rather like a queen receiving her subjects, until one got to know her and discovered what charm and what a wicked sense of humour she had. It was a great loss to the house when she decided to leave.' He gave a quick sigh, then smiled again. 'If she hasn't turned a corner of her new garden at Antibes into another sunlit refuge, then I'll eat my hat!'

All Lissa's instinctive liking for him at their former brief meeting in London had revived by this time, and she chose a particularly lovely Elizabeth of Glamis rose for his buttonhole.

'Have you been in France long, Mr Prentiss?' she asked.

'Oh, Max, please. We can't have all this formality now, you know. No, I've only been here a few days. There was some paper work and a few details to be settled in Paris, but the real reason I'm here, of course, and the most important thing, is the merger between Vaumonts' textiles firm and Fontaine, which will be finalised here this evening. Raoul has sent for me as one of the signatories to the contract. I have to leave straight after dinner, however, as I must be back in London tomorrow.'

The merger at last! Lissa finished arranging his buttonhole with fingers grown suddenly nerveless. Then she said in a voice she hardly recognised as her own, 'I didn't realise it would be so soon.'

'Negotiations have been proceeding for many months and Vaumonts are eager for the deal. I think they are not so strong financially as they would like the business world to believe,' he smiled at her. 'But they will suit our plans for expansion very well. And I have heard it said that there will be a merger of quite a different kind to be announced at the same time.'

Lissa murmured something incoherent in reply, her thoughts in a whirl. No matter what the Comtesse thought, Raoul seemed to be determined to tread the bitter path he had chosen for himself. Marriage to Dominique was part of the package deal he had arranged with Vaumonts. She shivered a little and Max looked at her with concern.

'Is it getting chilly, my dear? Perhaps you should have brought a wrap, but it was so sheltered on the terrace.'

'No, I'm quite warm, thank you. You know the old saying—a grey goose must have walked over my grave.' Lissa gave a determinedly bright smile. 'I'm so glad to see you here, Max. I'm going back to London with Maggie next week and we would probably never have met again.'

'Oh, I can't believe that,' he said. 'Surely you haven't forgotten your promise to visit Fontaine in London and see the fabric showrooms as we arranged? I can still remember the ones we thought would suit you best,' he said.

'That's very kind,' Lissa replied with a show of enthusiasm, but inwardly she was vowing she would never knowingly set foot on an inch of Fontaine territory again.

'Midsummer Night. That was the one,' Max said delightedly.

'Yes,' Lissa acknowledged, bending to pull the dead head off a rose to disguise the betraying colour in her face. 'I have actually seen a sample, and it was as beautiful as I had imagined.'

'Raoul has something even better up his sleeve these days. He and Nicole have been working together on a fabric that no one has been allowed even to catch a glimpse of. That's one reason I think she is here now, to put the finishing touches to it and make sure the creation is perfect as she planned it. It's been rushed into production already, I know.'

Lissa stared at a glowing mass of Peace roses, but there was no answering peace in her heart.

She knew what Max Prentiss was referring to. She could recall that mass of ivory with its shimmering silver tracery of the very flowers that were filling the air with their scent even then. Jour des Noces. Wedding day, she thought, being rushed through so that Dominique can wear it when the marriage in the little church in the village is solemnised. And afterwards there will be dancing in the square with the villagers, and Raoul will hold her in his arms.

She looked at Max, and forced a smile. 'You're right, it is getting a little cold. Shall we go back?'

As she dressed for dinner that night, Lissa's thoughts were in turmoil and her usually deft hands could not manage the elaborate chignon style she had chosen, so she merely tied it back loosely in a mass of waves with a piece of chiffon which matched the deep sapphire of her dress.

How could she stay and face the evening, knowing what it would bring? She knew from the conversation over afternoon tea that as well as the family lawyers, Dominique's parents, Monsieur and Madame Vaumont, were expected as dinner guests.

'It will be quite an occasion,' Madame de Gue said gaily. 'It is something that Fontaine has planned and hoped for for so long now.'

Lissa had also managed to have a quiet word with Paul before they separated to dress for dinner, and had thanked him for telling his mother the truth at last, and he flushed uncomfortably.

'It was foolish to go on, especially now when Raoul's marriage is a certainty. There has been discussion over settlements as well as the merger, I know, and he has sent the family jewels to Paris to be cleaned, so an announcement must come at any time. Besides,' he looked younger and more boyish than Lissa had ever seen him, 'there is Nicole.'

'I thought there might be,' Lissa said drily. She was faintly amused in spite of her own misery. 'Off with the new love and on with the old again,' she thought.

'We have known each other since we were children together,' Paul explained. 'We fell in love—but it was just a boy and girl affair, or so I thought. Then I met Dominique. She was like a butterfly, while my Nicole was most like a small quiet moth. I admit I was captivated.'

He paused, with a little sigh. 'I knew I was hurting Nicole, and the family who wanted us to marry, and I also knew I was making a fool of myself with Dominique. I always knew at the bottom of my heart what she was really like. But she is—exciting, and that was what I wanted then. But I never thought of marrying her. *Hélas*, she thought otherwise.'

'And then I came into the picture,' Lissa supplied

without rancour.

'Ah, no, never think that. I loved you truly, in my way, as I told you many times.'

'But your way wasn't mine, which is just as well. I think I was really an escape for you from Dominique.'

Paul looked abashed. '*Peut-être*,' he admitted at last. 'But only a little. I did care for you.'

Lissa kissed him on the cheek. 'Don't be unhappy,' she said gently. 'Nicole will make you very happy, and I have my own life in London to pick up again. There's the book to finish, and Jenny's wedding to look forward to. These weeks here have been an experience for me.'

Though not one she ever wanted to repeat, she added inwardly.

'Well, I may have escaped Dominique as a wife, only to be saddled with her as a *belle-sœur*,' Paul said with a groan, and Lissa felt a fresh pang of pain.

'You can't win them all,' she said in a voice that was barely audible even to herself, and they parted.

Later as she stood by her mirror, adjusting the silver ear-rings she was to wear with her dress, she was only too conscious of the shadows beneath her eyes and the lines of strain etching themselves about her mouth. She smiled experimentally, but it was a poor imitation of her usual gaiety, and looked strained and artificial. She would look tired and jaded against Dominique's triumphant bloom, she thought unhappily.

The salon was crowded when she entered, as she was the last down. Max Prentiss spotted her and brought her a dry martini, and it was he who introduced her to the Vaumonts, a short voluble couple, Madame already over-plump with masses of rings on her rather stubby fingers and brooches glittering on her prominent brocaded bosom.

Raoul, dark and saturnine in evening dress, was standing by the mantelpiece talking to Dominique, who was striking in an emerald-coloured gown that fitted her almost perfect figure like a second skin. The ideal background for the de Gue emeralds, Lissa supposed.

She joined Anne-Marie and Nicole, who had an air of suppressed joyousness about her and was wearing a charming dress in peacock blue which made her look more assured and less vulnerable. Lissa was glad to relax in their company.

Anne-Marie grimaced. 'I suppose the official announcement of the merger will be made during dinner. There will be speeches that will be *insupport-able*.' She grinned at Lissa. 'But at least there will be no bombshell as there was when your engagement was announced to Paul. Some time you must tell me all about that. I still haven't managed to think out what game you were both playing. At least this time we know what to expect. Vaumont textiles will at last belong to Fontaine.'

She lowered her voice a little. 'I am glad that you were not really engaged to Paul, *chérie*, and are not going to marry him. You would not have suited one another at all.'

Lissa flushed. 'I think you're right.'

Anne-Marie studied her curiously, then sighed. 'But in a way it is a pity. I would like you as my *belle-sœur*.' She gave her cousin a quick hug. 'But I would also like Nicole.'

Nicole was blushing to the roots of her hair and murmuring a quiet protest when Lissa felt a hand on her arm. She looked up and saw that Raoul was standing next to her.

'I should like a private word with you, *s'il vous plaît*,' he said quietly. 'The terrace will do.'

'Private words are difficult on public occasions like this. I think your absence even for a minute or two would be noticed and remarked on. Anyway, I think we have had more than enough to say to each other in the past.'

'*Au contraire*, there are a number of points still to be straightened out between us before I permit you to board that plane with Madame Desmond next week.'

'I do not require your permission to leave this house, *monsieur*, or take myself off anywhere that my fancy dictates. Please remember that. I am not one of your feudal vassals. Now Mademoiselle Vaumont is looking at us. No doubt she feels neglected, tonight of all nights.'

He turned abruptly and walked away. Lissa sank down on a small brocaded chair and tried to take a firm control of her confused emotions. One thing was clear—she could not sit through that dinner party now at any price, even if the other guests considered her ill-mannered or not.

Making her way to Madame, she made an excuse about a sudden attack of migraine, and was immediately made to feel guilty by the instant sympathetic response. '*Pauvre petite! Si pale!*' She declined the offers of tablets and a maid to sit with her until the attack wore off, or even a further visit from the doctor.

'*Merci, madame.*' She was aware of Raoul de Gue's cynical stare, and raised her voice a little. 'A little rest is all I need.'

After a brief word with Anne-Marie, she made her way to the door, which was opened for her by Max Prentiss, who had overheard her conversation with the Comtesse, and looked genuinely upset and disappointed.

'Not leaving us so soon, surely?' he said. 'I'd hoped to be in Paris myself next week, so perhaps I can show

178

you and Mrs Desmond Fontaine's Paris house as you will be passing through on your way home. And don't forget we have a date in London, if I don't see you before I leave tonight. I'd like you to meet Helen, my wife, and the kids too. But I can always contact you through Mrs Desmond, and I'll really try and fix up the Paris visit.'

Lissa looked up at him, barely registering what he was saying, although her lips formed mechanical thanks. A sudden inspiration had come to her. After all, he had said in the garden that he had to leave almost at once, and now he was talking about tonight.

'Are you leaving after dinner, Max?'

'I'm afraid so. I've packed already. This has really been a flying visit.'

This was her chance. She looked at him, summoning all her appeal. 'Max, when you leave for Paris tonight, will you take me with you? I desperately need to get to the airport, and a lift with you would solve all my problems.' Or at least some of them, she thought, choking back the tears that persisted in remaining so near the surface.

'A lift?' He stared at her, pushing his glasses up his forehead in a manner Lissa would have found faintly comical if she had not felt so distraught. 'But you're leaving with Mrs Desmond in a few days anyway. She mentioned this to me while we were having cocktails just now, and ...'

'I would prefer to leave tonight—after dinner, if that can be arranged. I have money and my passport, and I haven't very much luggage that I need to take. I can arrange to have my other things sent on later. Oh, Max, please help me. If I can just get to Paris I'm sure I can get a flight to London without too much difficulty.'

London, where Jenny would be waiting with Roger

and their wedding plans, and the sort of life that went smoothly like a breeze over summer meadows and did not challenge you to defy it. Where she could forget the scent of roses in a walled garden where she had dreamed dreams that were impossible about a man who had let bitterness and cynicism build a high wall around his heart.

Max Prentiss regarded her in silence for a moment. 'And once in London, what then?' he asked.

'I shall go down to Devon to visit my parents for a few days, and relax completely for a while. I—I've just let myself get thoroughly overtired, that's all.'

'I suppose it doesn't sound such a bad idea,' he said thoughtfully. 'Some sea air and good food should put some of the flesh back on your bones and the colour in your cheeks. If that is the only remedy, of course, and I confess I have my doubts about that.'

'Max, please will you take me with you?' Lissa was urgent.

'If you're sure that's what you want—and more important, what you need, my dear—then I'll take you.'

'I'm sure,' she said, and tried to smile. 'Bless you!'

Once in her room, she packed a single case with necessities. She was glad of the occupation to take her mind off the scene being enacted in the dining room below, but a tight knot of misery welled up inside her when she came upon the Fontaine-wrapped parcel of Midsummer Night, where she had hidden it at the back of the wardrobe. Tightening her lips, she took it out and laid it on the bed. She would not take it with her.

Then she wrote a brief note for Maggie, explaining why she could not stay any longer at the chateau once Raoul and Dominique were officially engaged, and left it on her godmother's dressing table. It was almost like an elopement, she thought wryly.

She changed into dark slim-fitting trousers which flared slightly at the ankles and topped them with a dark roll-necked sweater and a cream suede coat, then collecting her case and shoulder bag she crept out of the room. But in the corridor she paused and put her case down. She had forgotten one vital thing. She went back across the bedroom to the window and pulled back the curtains. The room was dark and she could just make out the outlines of the little walled garden.

And when the roses on Raoul's desk faded and the petals fell, would he allow Françoise to renew them, or would he treat the whole incident as if it had never happened, and leave the garden to run to waste again or become the sophisticated swimming pool of Dominique's desires?

In the gallery above the hall she waited. Dinner was over by now, she knew, and she could hear voices coming from the *petit salon*, Dominique's much in evidence. After about five minutes the door opened and Max Prentiss appeared and climbed the stairs towards her.

'You're ready then? Good girl,' he said. 'Give me ten minutes to collect my stuff and I'll take it out the back way and bring the car round to the front. I'll sound the horn once. O.K.?'

Lissa nodded gratefully, and he pointed to one of the many alcoves on the gallery, each with its looped-back curtain. 'If danger threatens, fair maiden, conceal yourself in there.'

Lissa laughed, and felt some of her tension lift as she did so. She sat down on one of the many brocaded chairs and glanced at her watch, suspecting that this was going to be the longest ten minutes of her life.

She looked around at the statuary and the paintings and the small staircases leading from the gallery which had seemed such a labyrinth when she had first arrived weeks ago, and which were now so familiar. She thought of the horses in the stables who would be waiting for her arrival early next day with their usual titbits.

A sob tore in her throat, quenched by the sudden unmistakable sound of a car's horn. He had been quicker than he thought, obviously.

She went noiselessly down the broad sweep of staircase and opened the big door. The car, long and dark in a night when hurrying clouds obscured the moon, waited on the gravel sweep at the foot of the wide stone steps. The sidelights were on, and the boot had been left open for her suitcase, she noticed. She loaded her case into it, then came round to the passenger door, only retaining her shoulder bag. The door was already open for her and she climbed in and slammed it shut, before turning to thank Max Prentiss.

'*Bon soir*,' said Raoul.

For a moment, Lissa could neither think nor speak. Then she gasped, knowing how idiotic it would sound, 'What are you doing here?'

'You required a chauffeur. I am happy to offer my services. Max has decided that a later flight will do for him after all, so here I am.'

'Let me out of this car!' Lissa demanded between clenched teeth.

'Never in this world—until we reach our destination. No'—as she made a sudden grab for the handle—'don't try and let yourself out. It is self-locking and can only be released now from the outside. Besides, you were so determined to have a lift in this car. Don't you trust my driving?'

He let in the clutch and the car moved smoothly off down the wide drive.

Lissa was shaking with temper and frustration. 'And what does your fiancée think of this latest little escapade of yours, or has she agreed to turn a blind eye already?'

'You seem very determined to marry me off,' he commented. 'Which fiancée is this?'

Lissa stared at him. 'Tonight—the merger with Vaumont Textiles. You know what I mean. Paul refused to marry her, so it was left to you...' Her voice trailed away.

'The merger with Vaumonts was signed well before dinner—which, incidentally, you were fortunate to miss. Old Vaumont made a speech of the most *formidable* which almost sent our good Max to sleep.'

'But I thought part of it was to be...' Lissa could not go on.

'You thought part of the bargain was Dominique. And I must confess it was my fault that you thought so. That was what I wanted to tell you tonight, among other things, when you came into the salon like a brave little ghost with your blue dress and your trinkets and that lost look which makes me forget everything but the desire to hold you in my arms.'

Lissa stared at him. 'Then you are truly not engaged to Dominique?'

'Heaven forbid!' he said fervently, then he began to laugh. 'And I will also pledge that having said so, I will not reverse my decision during the next twenty-four hours, as you did with Paul.'

He gave her a slanting smile. 'And neither is Paul engaged to her either. That was never part of my plan.'

'But he told me...'

'Oh, I know what he told you. Dynastic marriages and other nonsense that went out with the Dark Ages you seem to think I belong to. *Quelle bêtise!* And to think I was responsible! Maman, the whole family want Paul to marry Nicole. It has been the dream of our hearts since they were children. But suddenly he begins to philander with little money-grabbers like Dominique, and young English women with doubtful reputations,' he added with a sideways grin. 'So what is one to do? In a moment of madness I gave him an ultimatum—marry Dominique or else—hoping he would recover his senses and return to Nicole, who has never ceased to love him, *la pauvre*.'

'But instead he turned to me,' Lissa said slowly.

They were through the village now, driving at a steady pace. Raoul shot her a glance. 'I did not bargain for that after you had told me that night on the terrace that there was no engagement. Why did you change your mind?'

Lissa was glad of the darkness of the car to hide her crimson cheeks. 'I came to the library and heard you talking on the telephone. You said that Paul's little affair had been settled and it hadn't cost a sou. I thought you meant you had got rid of me without having to buy me off.'

Raoul brought the car to the side of the road, braked and switched off the engine.

'So that was it,' he said softly. 'I knew there was something. What I was telling Anne-Marie, as it happens, was that I had put an end to whatever feeling Paul had for Dominique by ordering their marriage, and that there was no danger as far as I could see of the merger being jeopardised. The Vaumonts are too practical in business matters for that. Besides, Dominique has plenty of other irons in the fire. God help the one she chooses. For a time, I believe she thought it was me, but that was only her opinion, *hélas*.'

He reached out for her in the darkness. 'And how will you salvage my wounded pride? I was about to announce our own engagement at dinner, having proposed to you most romantically in Madame Grand'-

mère's garden, and then my fiancée-to-be arranges to run away from me with a business associate who has the good sense to tell me what she is planning, praise be to *le bon Dieu.*'

'But I thought you hated me for deceiving you about Paul,' Lissa said numbly, hardly able to take in what he had just said.

He laid a finger caressingly on her lips. 'I told you once before, *ma belle,* you did not deceive me. That engagement to Paul was far too convenient. Besides, a woman can lie with words, but not with her eyes, or with her body, and each time I held you, I knew the truth—that you wanted me as much as I want you. Isn't it so, Lissa, *ma bien-aimée?*'

He bent his head and his lips found hers, gently at first and then with a growing insistence, until her own parted beneath his, and she was clinging to him, all her inhibitions swept away, longing only to belong to him completely, revelling in the intimate touch of his hands as he caressed her, his hands expertly drawing fire from every contour of her slim body.

At last it was Raoul who reluctantly pulled away.

'Not here. Not yet,' he said, with a faint smile. 'I still have the *droit du seigneur*, you know, and we have already discussed the conditions for that.'

'You know too much about women,' Lissa murmured, feeling a slight pang of jealousy at the thought of all the others with whom he had gained his undoubted expertise.

He put his finger under her chin, tilting it so that he could look into her eyes.

'There have been women in my life, Lissa. I won't lie to you or pretend that I have lived as a monk before I married Victoire, or after. But there will never again be anyone but you, I swear it.' He lifted her fingers to his lips and kissed them. A strange stillness

185

filled the car, and Lissa felt sudden tears prick her eyelids.

'And now I have your consent to our marriage,' he
silenced her gasp of protest with another kiss, then
traced a lazy path with his lips down her throat to the
confines of her collar, 'I will give you your wedding
present.'

He reached into the back seat of the car and produced a large flat parcel in the familiar Fontaine
wrapping paper, tied with white ribbons. Lissa stared
at it for a moment in silence, then with trembling fingers she unfastened the ribbons and slid the paper
aside, staring entranced as the ivory and silver folds of
Jour des Noces poured into her lap, the silver roses
gleaming like gossamer in the interior light of the car
which Raoul had switched on for her.

'You like it?' he asked. 'I thought, like Grand'mère,
you would prefer a flower design, and what better
than the roses you have brought back to life in her
garden—your garden now, *ma mie*, where you will sit
and wait for our little ones to be born and play with
them when they are older.'

'And Françoise?' Lissa almost breathed the question.

'And Françoise. *Ma petite* Françoise. She will be our
eldest and have a special place in our lives,' he said
quietly. 'Thanks to you, *ma chère*, who had more
wisdom than I. Poor Victoire! How she must have
hated me to have told me such a lie.'

Lissa took his hand and laid it to her cheek. 'We
won't talk about it any more. It's gone now, in the past
for ever.'

His mouth found hers again, but this time with a
kind of gratitude and wonder mingled with the passion.

As he released her, Lissa began to carefully re-wrap

the folds of Jour de Noces on her knee. 'I thought this was meant for Dominique,' she confessed.

'How wise in some ways, my sweet one, and how foolish in others. If you knew the strings I have had to pull, the rush there has been to get the material ready in time. It has been altogether *formidable*.'

He leaned back in the seat, watching her re-tying the ribbon.

'*Eh bien, alors,*' he said lazily. 'What became of that other material I gave you? The Midsummer Night which seems to have become your own individual design, according to Max and Nicole.'

'I left it in my room,' Lissa told him. 'I swore I would never accept it.'

He laughed. 'Well, it can be rescued. You can dine in it on our wedding night and wear it to the festivities in the village afterwards.'

'You're so sure I mean to marry you,' Lissa murmured provocatively.

'I'm sure I mean to marry you or I will not be answerable for the consequences,' he told her. 'Do you think I can ever forget the glory of your skin against mine, *ma belle*? And that was merely a taste. Even a veiling of Midsummer Night will be too much of an intrusion once you are really mine, so be warned.'

Lissa's cheeks were warm, but she was not afraid. 'I don't think I need warning,' she told him candidly, and stroked his face where the high cheekbone showed tautly through his tanned skin.

'Do that again, *ma belle*, and I warn you I shall anticipate our midsummer night here and now,' he said. 'If you wish to be safe from me and useful at the same time, you can navigate.'

He drew a leatherbound book of road maps from the glove compartment and tossed it into her lap.

'Navigate?' Lissa stared at him. 'But you must know

187

your way to Paris like the back of your hand.'

'*Certainement*—if Paris was our destination. But we are going to Antibes, *ma chérie*, to introduce Madame Grand'mère to yet another English bride. She is especially anxious to meet the girl who has brought her dreaming garden back to life, and restored it to a place where dreams can come true.'

Lissa laughed, a sound of pure joy. 'And to think I told Maggie I would leave the Chateau without a backward glance!'

He smiled, brushing his fingers across his lips, then pressing them to hers as the car slid forward.

'And so you shall, Lissa. From now on, we will not look back, but only forward to the joy we shall have together.'

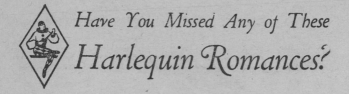

# *Have You Missed Any of These*
# *Harlequin Romances?*

## Have You Missed Any of These
# Harlequin Romances?

**All books listed 75c**

---

Harlequin Romances are available at your local bookseller,
or through the Harlequin Reader Service, M.P.O. Box 707,
Niagara Falls, N.Y. 14302; Canadian address: 649 Ontario St.,
Stratford, Ontario  N5A 6W4.

# Harlequin Presents..

All books listed are available at **95c each** at your local bookseller or through the Harlequin Reader Service.

---

**TO: HARLEQUIN READER SERVICE, Dept. N 601**
**M.P.O. Box 707, Niagara Falls, N.Y. 14302**
**Canadian address: Stratford, Ont., Can. N5A 6W4**

☐ Please send me the free Harlequin Romance Presents Catalogue.

☐ Please send me the titles checked.

I enclose $................ (No C.O.D.s). All books listed are 95c each. To help defray postage and handling cost, please add 25c.

Name ................................................................

Address ................................................................

City/Town ................................................................

State/Prov. ........................... Postal Code...............

X

*Have you missed any of these . . .*

## Harlequin Presents..

**All books listed 95c**

Harlequin Presents novels are available at your local bookseller, or through the Harlequin Reader Service, M.P.O. Box 707, Niagara Falls, N.Y. 14302; Canadian address: 649 Ontario St., Stratford, Ontario N5A 6W4.